Waiting for Deliverance

Betsy Urban

Orchard Books • New York

To Dad,
for Parshallburg

ACKNOWLEDGMENTS
My thanks to readers Deb Scheffler, Joe Urban, and Kathy Urban
for early advice and encouragement. A special thanks to Rebecca
Davis for her gracious editing. —B.U.

The Publisher gratefully thanks Ms. Stephanie Betancourt of the
National Museum of the American Indian, Smithsonian Institution,
for her kind assistance.

Orchard Books
95 Madison Avenue, New York, NY 10016

Manufactured in the United States of America
Book design by Vicki Fischman
The text of this book is set in 14.5 point Bembo.
10 9 8 7 6 5 4 3 2 1

Library of Congress Cataloging-in-Publication Data
Urban, Betsy.
Waiting for Deliverance / by Betsy Urban.
    p.   cm.
Summary: In 1793 orphaned fourteen-year-old Livy and her cousin,
Ephraim, are taken in by a backcountry farmer and his family, including
a young Seneca man who changes Livy's attitudes toward the Indians she
was raised to hate and fear.
ISBN 0-531-30310-1 (trade : alk. paper)
ISBN 0-531-33310-8 (library : alk. paper)
[1. Frontier and pioneer life—New York (State)—Fiction. 2. Seneca
Indians—Fiction. 3. Indians of North America—New York (State)—
Fiction. 4. Prejudices—Fiction. 5. Orphans—Fiction. 6. New York
(State)—Fiction.] I. Title.
PZ7.U635 Wai 2000   [Fic]—dc21   00-24218

Historical Note

It is 1793, a time when western New York is still part of the American frontier. The Revolutionary War ended in 1784, but conflicts among the peoples in this region have continued.

The Seneca Indians had sided with the British in the American Revolution, only to be abandoned by their former ally afterward. Although the Seneca and other Iroquois nations had driven settlers from New York's western frontier with relentless guerrilla warfare, the British left all mention of the Indians out of the treaty that ended the war. This came as a shock to the Indians. They had gained territory and won their corner of the war, but the Americans acted like conquerors.

After the Revolution, American settlers bought up former Seneca land in the Finger Lakes region of upstate New York. To the west of the remaining Seneca territory, some of the Ohio Valley was being settled legally, but many frontiersmen simply seized land that belonged to the western tribes. The tribes reacted, and war erupted on the frontiers of Pennsylvania, Kentucky, and Ohio. Even in New York there were isolated confrontations that left both Senecas and Americans dead.

In the early 1790s, Seneca chief Cornplanter urged peace at Indian councils held on the Maumee and Glaize Rivers. It was a wise course of action for the Seneca Nation, caught between the Americans and the warring tribes. Then, in Ohio in 1791, the western tribes destroyed half of American general Arthur St. Clair's army in Ohio. Encouraged by this victory, they pressured Cornplanter to join them. He refused, but some young Seneca warriors had already joined, and even as Cornplanter tried to maintain a position of neutrality, they continued to fight.

In March of 1793, the frontier of western New York is now rife with rumors. The American settlers hate the British in Upper Canada, who they think are helping the western tribes. British spies are active, and the forts at Niagara and Detroit are still under British control. Across the young nation, the major news event is the Indian war on the frontier.

Despite this atmosphere of suspicion, uncertainty, and fear, settlers continue to pour into New York's western frontier. Our story begins as two of them, young Deliverance and Ephraim Pelton, find themselves destitute and alone in the tiny village of Vienna.

For more historical information, please see the glossary at the end of this book.

Waiting for Deliverance

Chapter 1

Deliverance Pelton surveyed the gathering of men and boys cautiously from the recesses of her borrowed sunbonnet. The brim was too wide. When she dropped her chin, it shuttered her face so completely that a young farmer wanting to get a look startled her by gripping both sides and peering in as if she were at the bottom of a sack.

She had been to auctions before, although never to one held in a tavern. Back home in Conway, Massachusetts, Uncle John had taken her to the October stock show for as long as she could remember. She was a good judge of cattle and oxen. But this was her first experience with a Pauper's Auction, and it was her first experience of being for sale.

Even after two weeks, the horror of the accident—of her little cousins and aunt and uncle being swept away in the river—wouldn't leave her. One moment she was bundling the baby into a warmer shift and wondering at the flatboat's sudden tilt; the next, she was up to her neck in icy water, and the baby was gone. Sorrow intruded hourly. Sometimes she could hear the river roar, though it was a quarter mile distant from the Wilkeses' house, where they were boarded. No one else heard, and Mrs. Wilkes would touch her gently to bring her back. It embarrassed her and made her blush with shame, knowing that she and her cousin Ephraim were a burden. No Pelton had been a charge on the county since their ancestors arrived in Boston in 1637. The only consolation was that they were on the western frontier in New York, and no one from Conway would see.

"Marry the girl off. Save the village of Vienna some revenue and warm a poor widower's bed into the bargain. It's been uncommon cold this spring, Wilkes," Mayor Borst said as he ducked his head and peered into Livy's face.

The Peltons were austere people with a gift for composure, or the appearance of it. Nonetheless, being discussed as if she were deaf and dumb and stared at so intently was almost more than Livy could bear. Ephraim, seated next to her on the bench, gave her hand a squeeze. Grief had softened him.

Mayor Borst wiped his mouth with a grubby hand. This girl didn't look particularly warm to him. Typical Yankee most likely. Here it was, two weeks since she and the boy had been rescued from the crack-up on the Canandaigua Outlet, and she looked as if she hadn't even started to thaw.

"Take off that bonnet, child," he commanded.

Livy loosened the strings and let it fall back. Mayor Borst got a brief look at her face before she went back to studying her shoes. Her eyes were the color of storm clouds, and her face was pale. At the mention of marriage, her lips had clamped shut, setting her chin stubbornly.

"Now then, little missy. Why don't you stand up so's I can get a good look at you."

Livy bristled at the title, *missy. Miss* was a reprimand reserved for the ill-tempered and the disobedient. She was neither, and no one, stranger or relation, had ever addressed her with anything less than a *missus.* She glanced over at Mr. Wilkes, justice of the peace, overseer for the poor, and their temporary guardian. He nodded. The mayor was an unschooled frontiersman, so Mr. Wilkes made allowances, but his rueful look was the same one Livy saw him direct at his wife's back a hundred times a week.

Reluctantly she stood, clutching Ephraim's hand behind her back.

"How old are you, gal?"

"Fourteen, sir," she said with a curtsy. The Pelton children had been raised to "make their manners" to all adults, no matter how lowly. Livy was sure these were the lowliest she had ever seen.

Aunt Mary had been right to oppose the move west, not that Uncle John ever listened to her.

Livy raised her eyes to the sooty hearth. Smoke, damp, cold, and filth. She wanted to be home in Conway, in her own cozy bed under the eaves, under the comforter with the coverlet she had woven herself, safe and warm. She closed her eyes for a moment, willing it, but the old man was still there when she opened them.

"It's sad to see a young'un so dour and forlorn. Don't help her looks none, neither. You know what I always say, Wilkes, get 'em young and train 'em proper, like a huntin' dog. Marry her off." Mayor Borst smiled at her, showing tobacco-stained teeth set in pale gums, while a murmur of agreement ran through the crowd. Livy cringed as faces turned toward her, but Mr. Wilkes shook his head at the mayor's suggestion.

"She's too young."

"Not for little Ollie Rhodes. He's barely nineteen hisself. Lost his wife last winter. He could use a new one," the mayor said, winking at Livy.

"He didn't lose her," Mr. Wilkes said grimly. "He sold her to a trader in Canandaigua for one dollar."

"A dollar?"

"None of the parties complained of the arrangement." Mr. Wilkes glanced at his watch. "That Rhodes boy is more savage than Christian."

"Awful warm girl to go for only a dollar," the mayor said. "Now this one, a dollar's about all you'll get." He leaned back, resting his tankard on his belly. "When's your birthday, missy?"

"August."

He raised his tankard in a salute. "She is a bit puny though, Wilkes. Have her lift her skirt some. Just to her knees."

Livy went hot all over. She'd heard of people catching fire from their own shame and misery and burning to cinders.

"You're drunk, Luther," Mr. Wilkes said quietly.

"She ain't got no muscle in her arm. What good's a servant girl can't handle a sickle at haying? Now, if she's got muscle in her legs, she might make a fair plowgirl. If I'm gonna bid on her, I got a right to know." Some of the crowd laughed.

"If you were to bid on her, Luther, I wouldn't let you have her. You're a widower. She goes to a God-fearing householder with a wife. This is not one of those Virginia slave auctions."

"Close enough," Ephraim whispered.

Widow Barnes, the only other pauper for sale that afternoon, tugged at Livy's skirt. "Sit you down, deary. He's only teasing. It's his way of cheering you up, the old fool." She spat the words and gave him a sour look.

"It wouldn't surprise me if they stripped us naked and looked at our teeth," Ephraim said by way of comfort.

Widow Barnes thumped his head. "Nonsense." She turned to Livy. "You'll do fine, dearie. A nice little lady like you. They's saying you spin and weave like a woman grown and"—she paused in her wonder at it—"that you can read and write. Imagine that. They won't be givin' *you* to no old man for a belly warmer. You can put that notion right out of your head."

Livy drew the faded sunbonnet over her face. The linsey-woolsey overgown Mrs. Wilkes had given her served to swallow the rest of her. Her fingers played nervously with a frayed sleeve. During the first painful days after the accident, there had been talk of returning her and Eph to Massachusetts. She had prayed hard for it, but, with planting about to commence, no one could be found willing to travel east. Her disappointment had turned to despair when Mr. Wilkes got the idea of binding Eph to a road crew that was building a road to link the settlements. Thankfully, eleven years old was deemed too young to fell trees, and that scheme was abandoned.

Ephraim was engaged in a staring match with a farmer's son. His expression was insolent, and several of the men who saw the look determined not to bid. "Eph, please," Livy whispered. "We'll be separated sure if you keep on making faces. They'll think you're troublesome. Just remember Mrs. Wilkes." At this rebuke Eph dropped his eyes. Early on, Mr. Wilkes had proposed taking both Livy and Ephraim, but Mrs. Wilkes had said, "Laggard. Keep the girl if you like. I've no objection to her, but that boy's a waste. We've no room for laziness."

"Did you inherit anything, boy?" the mayor asked abruptly.

Eph pretended not to hear. It was his way of dealing with unpleasantness.

"Yes, sir," Livy said quickly. "Six hundred wilderness acres, soldier's right. My Uncle John and my father were in the Sixth Massachusetts. Uncle John fought here with General Sullivan in 1779. It's bounty land."

"Well, she *can* talk." The mayor tried another grin on her, to no avail. "God bless 'em, missy. The Sixth were brave men, and them Seneca had it coming. It's just too bad they didn't slaughter the lot of 'em. But your uncle was confounded slow in claiming it. The war's been over ten years. In this market those six hundred acres will only sell for thirty-five dollars, if you're lucky and the title's good. It ain't right, but them's the facts."

"Actually, after probate and subtracting the village's expenses for their room and board, I'm afraid they will be penniless," Mr. Wilkes put in. "It's a shame your uncle left nothing with friends back home."

He hadn't. It was nothing Livy hadn't heard already. But she wasn't prepared for the mayor's next remark.

"The man was a fool."

Ephraim gasped at the words. As an only son, spoiled and as full of himself as a bantam rooster, he was short-tempered. He nearly went for the old man, but Livy stopped him with a quick boot to his shin. Eph squawked just as the door opened and a curious figure stepped in.

Livy had never seen a man dressed in skins before. In the flickering firelight, they matched his weathered face and made him seem all of a piece, like a tree trunk. His ancient hunting shirt of scratched and greasy deerskin hung to his knees. The hem was ragged and uneven. His moccasins and leggings were coated with dried mud that dropped to the floor like dirty rain when he turned to close the door. Livy saw long, dark hair glistening with grease and tied with a string. There was a hatchet in his belt and a rifle in his hand. He had a couple of heavy elm-bark packs that he laid carefully against the wall.

He crossed to the hearth, and when he found the chairs occupied and no one inclined to share a bench, he sank easily to the hearthstone about ten inches from Livy's feet, holding his hands to the fire. As she watched him furtively, he pulled a knife from within his shirt and began to scrape at the mud on his moccasins.

The men seated closest to the ragged figure at the fireside were agitated. Livy heard someone whisper, "Scalping knife!" and the conversation died completely.

"Any knife's a scalping knife," the newcomer said, "if you know where to cut." He fixed his eyes on the young farmer who had spoken. The young man started up, as if to answer, but his companion laid a restraining hand on his shoulder. The newcomer smiled coldly and went back to grooming himself. He turned his head and caught Livy studying him. His expression was unfriendly, and she looked away, mortified.

A voice from the back of the room broke the silence. "It's a tragedy. Whoever sold 'em that flatboat this time of year had an obligation to tell 'em about the high water. Should have warned him off. Them with six children and all."

"They was warned," the mayor said quietly.

To her shame, Livy remembered the warning and her uncle's reaction to it. He had hired three men on the Seneca River to pole for him. When the water rose on Canandaigua Outlet, they tied up the flatboat. They told him to wait it out for a week or two. "They just want a week's idleness at our expense," he told Aunt Mary. He dismissed the men and went on without them. Two hours later he was dead, Aunt Mary and the little girls with him.

The mayor went on. "Stubborn jackass. Should have sledded in last winter with the rest of those New Englanders 'stead of going it alone. Yankee know-it-all. Present company excepted, of course, Wilkes."

The children colored hotly, and Livy threw her arm around Ephraim's waist, pinning him to the settle.

Mr. Wilkes ignored the mayor's remark and addressed the

crowd. "These goods here"—he indicated the tools and a patched-up flax wheel set on the stone floor—"are all that were salvaged from the river. They are open to bid. The little maid is an accomplished spinster and weaver, experienced with children, and very capable in a household. Mrs. Wilkes has been favorably impressed." There was a murmur of approval. "And the boy . . . is used to farmwork. Both can read and write a legible hand, so you won't have schooling expenses. The village is conducting this auction New England style. You must bid what you calculate your monthly costs will be to feed and clothe the pauper. Lowest bid wins. The village will pay for their upkeep on an annual basis."

"Need the young'uns go together, sir?"

Mr. Wilkes avoided looking at the children as he said, "No."

Livy's hopes sank as surely as a rock dropped in a river.

"It would be fine to keep them in the same household, but we must be realistic. And mind your bids, gentlemen. Should expenses prove to be more than anticipated, there will be no increase."

"I knew it!" Eph whispered. "He lied to us, Livy." She felt his trembling and fought to control her own. She could hide her hands behind her back, but not her face. She couldn't allow her lips to tremble, or she'd cry and shame them both.

"It's a small village," she whispered slowly, her own words sounding distant to her. "We'll see each other, every day probably. Isn't that right, ma'am?"

Widow Barnes smiled and nodded. No point in telling the poor things that many of the tracts were as large as their worthless six hundred acres.

"Put the spinster up first," someone shouted.

Mr. Wilkes turned to Livy. She saw him hold out his hand. It seemed as if he were miles away. "Come here, child," he said. "There's nothing to be afraid of."

Aunt Mary had been impatient with her excessive shyness. "It shows a remarkable vanity in an unremarkable child," she would scold. "No one ever pays you the slightest attention." Livy stood up.

There was a rude noise and a low whistle from some boys at the back of the room. An adult voice growled, "For shame!" but the rum and water had reached the bigger boys. They were in a merry mood and broke into snorts of laughter.

"Eph! Don't!" Livy cried out as Ephraim, fuming, started off the settle and into the crowd. Barely looking, the newcomer caught him by the waist and held him. Eph turned and sputtered at him, but the man only stared back.

The laughter ended with a loud *smack* as a farmer's callused hand slapped an ear. For an instant, the public room was absolutely silent. Livy felt her eyes fill with tears. " 'Your strength shall be equal to your day,' " she whispered, repeating Aunt Mary's favorite homily.

Mayor Borst waved his hand. "I bid ten shillings on the maid."

A haze surrounded Livy. The sound of boots scuffing on pine board seemed deafeningly loud. She had never fainted but thought maybe she was about to. The room was growing black, and there were sparks going off all around like shooting stars.

"No, Luther." Mr. Wilkes put a protective hand on Livy's shoulder, and the sparks went out.

The mayor looked hurt. "I need a housekeeper, Wilkes. I can assure you, I see no attraction in the little sourpuss." He smiled, and bowed elaborately at Livy as if he'd said something gallant. His tankard fell to the floor with a clang.

"I bid eight shillings," said a voice from the back of the room.

Then another: "I got a goose about her size. She can't be a big eater. Make it seven."

The crowd laughed. Livy repeated, "Your strength shall be equal to your day" over and over in her head.

A young farmer with a red nose and bleary eyes staggered up to her and bent to examine her face. She smelled rum and bad teeth.

"I'll take a kiss on trial, missus, if you don't object."

Before Mr. Wilkes could stop him, he'd pressed his mouth to hers. The next instant he was on the floor.

"She objects right well," the mayor shouted. "The chit's got muscle in her after all. What a blow!"

Livy recoiled as if she'd discharged her uncle's Kentucky rifle.

Mr. Wilkes caught her before she fell over, while the onlookers clapped and cheered. Before she regained her feet, the newcomer sprang up, putting himself between Livy and the downed man, raising a cloud of dirt and ashes in the process. The gentlemen who'd been lounging about him put a protective hand over their tankards.

"I bid a shilling a month, for the two of them."

The onlookers gasped. Mayor Borst laughed and said, "Gonna feed them on swamp muck and water, Gideon?"

Mr. Wilkes let go of Livy, and she ducked behind his back.

"You must mean a shilling apiece, Mr. Gunn," he said.

Gideon Gunn looked down at the floor, scratching at a week-old beard. "No, squire, I said a shilling. That's all I'll need, I reckon. We don't live high."

Peeking out at Mr. Gunn, Livy was suddenly aware of a peculiar odor. Even in a room full of men who wore work shirts stiff with dried sweat and tobacco spit, he was noticeable.

"Come now, Gideon. I have an auction to run, and it's near dusk. Sit down and stop making a nuisance of yourself."

Mr. Gunn sat down obediently but said, "I can only take the little'uns. No disrespect intended to you, ma'am"—he nodded to Widow Barnes—"but we have three babies now, and I doubt you'd be up to it. They take after their maw. A flighty bunch, ma'am. Stubborn, too."

"Gideon, please," Mr. Wilkes said.

"I'm a victim of bad timing, squire. My Pol's right spry for an overeducated female, but with a springtime babe she's no use to me."

The men sniggered. Gunn's woman had a fine figure and a marvelous, pretty face, but local mythology held that she was probably afflicted, else a simpleton like Gunn never could have won her. There was no danger of her being overeducated.

"I don't believe the village can refuse me, squire. No disrespect, but I got the same rights as any of you."

"Gideon, you're being ridiculous. You can't feed and clothe them on that. Why, you'd have to work them day and night to make it up."

Eph let out a groan.

Livy knew that being bound out to strangers would be uncomfortable at first, but at least the men gathered in the tavern seemed respectable. They wore the same tow shirts and trousers as her uncle, walked like farmers, talked like farmers, and used chairs when they sat down. Most of all, they didn't smell like heathen wildmen. She closed her eyes. That unfamiliar smell lodged in her throat, invaded her belly. Surely someone else would take them both. She couldn't bear being sent away with such a creature.

Mr. Gunn smiled, showing strong, white teeth. "You know I never work that hard, squire."

"He's a simpleton, Livy," Eph whispered.

"What do you say, squire? Polly could really use that girl. Not even one lady came to help her through the birthing. Not that I hold a grudge. It's a fair piece to travel, and the rain this spring's turned all the trails slimy, and you'd have to be Seneca, or a blame idiot, to go out on the rivers."

"One shilling a month?" Mr. Wilkes cocked his head to one side, eyeing Gideon Gunn like a greedy nuthatch contemplating suet.

Mr. Gunn nodded and put a hand to the back of his neck. Livy held her breath. Most folks she knew held that a sponge bath once a month was plenty until the weather turned warm. Even then, it was considered unhealthy to immerse your whole body, and in some places it was actually illegal. But she doubted Gideon Gunn saw soap from one end of the year to the next.

Mr. Gunn strolled over to Ephraim, who was glaring resentfully at his remark about idiots and rivers.

"Just how do you intend to church these children, Gideon Gunn?" Widow Barnes said, standing and settling knuckles the size of walnuts on her hips. "Seeing as how you and your little missus hain't managed to come to meetin' for your wedding or brought your babes for baptism, I would be interested in how you plan to teach these children their catechism."

Mr. Gunn was measuring his foot alongside Ephraim's.

"I'll learn 'em, Miz Barnes, the Bible . . . and how to mind their own business. They'll learn to get along so's they won't need to go troublin' folks with their upkeep"—he paused and flashed a smile at the old lady—"when they're older."

Widow Barnes gasped at the insult.

"Boy's anything like a puppy, with those feet, he'll grow six foot for sure," Mr. Gunn said cheerily, to no one in particular.

"Mr. Wilkes!" Widow Barnes's old chin was quivering. "These are careful-raised Christian children. You know it ain't right."

"There is a law involved, Mrs. Barnes. And it is my duty to uphold it. The law says the village must accept the lowest bid, and it appears . . ."

Mr. Wilkes looked hopefully at the crowd, but no one came forward. In early spring everyone was suffering through the six weeks' want, when food stores were nearly depleted and nature was still recovering from winter. Few could afford an extra mouth to feed.

"It appears Mr. Gunn has made it," Mr. Wilkes conceded.

Gideon Gunn, having completed his inspection of Ephraim, turned to Livy. She was relieved he didn't poke and prod at her as he had Eph.

"You don't look much like your brother," he said.

Livy was silent. Children did not banter with adults. Anyway, it was just the grown-up way of saying she was plain. What answer could she make to that?

Mr. Wilkes looked up from the papers he was preparing. "They're cousins," he said.

"Can you plant a kitchen garden and cook?" Mr. Gunn asked.
She nodded.

"Ever minded babies?"

Livy nodded and tried to put thoughts of her little cousins out of her head.

"Ever plow a field or help butcher a hog?"

Livy stopped nodding and wondered if he was fooling with her. Back home in Conway the menfolk did those things. Even farmers' daughters worked indoors most of the time.

He smiled at her confusion. "You don't say much, but better a silent woman than a magpie." To Livy's dismay he stuck out a filthy paw and chucked her on the chin. "Smile. You ain't going to your doom."

Ephraim was slouched in the settle, eyeing their new master resentfully as he bent over their papers, signing a large *X* in place of his name. "He did look at my teeth! He touched my mouth!" Eph grimaced and wiped his mouth with his fist.

Livy sat next to him as straight as a fence-post pine. "At least we'll be together, and that's all we hoped for. I suppose we'll get used to the rest."

"How, Livy? He's a simpleton."

"Don't be ornery."

"You're the ornery one. I thought you were going to snap his hand off."

"I hate being told to smile. It doesn't mean I'm not grateful. We're together, and that's all that matters."

"I promise I'll be good, Livy. We won't be parted because of me. But he's a peculiar one, isn't he? Doesn't even smell like a human being. Nor any animal I know, neither."

There was just a hint of admiration in his voice.

Chapter 2

Before retiring to the kitchen to take her supper with Eph, Livy helped Mrs. Wilkes serve the men a meager fish chowder with corn bread. Mr. Gunn paid Livy scant attention when she set a bowl before him. He sprawled opposite Mr. Wilkes, greasy elbows propped on the polished mahogany table, telling a story about a fur trappers' rendezvous that Livy couldn't understand but recognized as unsuitable. Mr. Wilkes forgot his dignity so far as to snort, then laugh out loud. Mrs. Wilkes sat down heavily, held a scented handkerchief to her nose, and declined the bread basket after Mr. Gunn plunged his hand into it. Imperiously, she shushed him for grace, but he went right on with his story afterward, eating noisily the whole time.

Livy lingered, sweeping ashes at the hearth, fascinated. He reminded her of Ezra Ottes back home. All the villages had men like Ezra. He'd spent time in the stocks and was even whipped publicly for disturbing the peace. He'd disappeared last winter, drunk under a snow drift as it turned out come February thaw.

Mr. Gunn finished his story about the fur trappers and started in on a Mr. Allen in Rochester who had three wives, simultaneously. This was too much for Mrs. Wilkes. "Mr. Gunn," she said, her double chin quivering in fury, "this is hardly a story suitable for adults, let alone a young lady. Livy Pelton, child, leave this room at once!"

Red-faced, Livy dropped a curtsy and scurried back to the kitchen. Ephraim looked up from his supper. "Ezra Ottes," Livy said in answer to his questioning look. "He's like Ezra Ottes, except he's not drunk. But not even Ezra was as uncouth as this . . . when he was sober."

It didn't ease Livy's mind any the next morning to have Mrs. Wilkes fussing over her. She tied and retied Livy's bonnet strings and even kissed Ephraim, whom she disliked heartily, good-bye. She was not speaking to her husband, and he took advantage of her silence to smoke a pipe at table, while she fumed. When the time finally came to part, she pressed a tightly wrapped parcel into Livy's hand.

"Mr. Gunn, I am giving this child a Bible that has been in my family for fifty years. My husband carried it through the French and Indian War, and the War for Independence. I am certain it saved his life on one occasion." She paused, and astonished Livy with an affectionate hug. "I want you to know that I expect the child to read to you and yours every Sabbath. Your household is very fortunate in acquiring children with such learning."

"Very kind of you, ma'am," Mr. Gunn said. "I'm sure it's kindly meant." There was a slight smile on his lips. "My Polly is right fond of hearing folks as can read." He clicked his heels like a soldier and gave Mrs. Wilkes a bow and a grin. Livy was almost sure he was sporting with the old lady, but no one else seemed amused.

Mr. Gunn was silent for their half-hour tramp through the woods. Even the birds were quiet, so that Livy heard the river long before she saw it. Her stomach tightened when the path came to an end on a steep bank looking down into the brown water. Reluctantly she and Ephraim followed Mr. Gunn a dozen steps down the slope to a large elm-bark canoe lying keel-up in the grass.

A young man emerged from the shadow of a sycamore tree to watch them approach. He smiled and waved a tawny hand. Livy had never laid eyes on an Indian before, but she'd grown up listening to her uncle's war stories. This creature was exactly as her uncle had described them. His head was shaven, nearly, except for a tangle of long, black hair gathered forward in a scalp lock displaying two feathers. There was a silver ring through his nose, and heavy silver disks weighed down his earlobes. He got to his feet, and even though he was wearing a homespun jacket, like the men at the tavern, underneath he wore the long calico shirt of a Seneca warrior. His leggings were blue broadcloth, his breechcloth scarlet, and on his feet he wore brightly beaded moccasins. There were silver brooches at his shoulder and along his sash, and an iron tomahawk tucked into his belt. Livy felt a shiver run down her back, forgot a late-night resolution to be courageous, and took a cowardly step behind Ephraim.

Mr. Gunn gripped the young man in a bear hug. They talked quietly a few moments, and once the young man gave Livy and Ephraim a level, appraising look. Then he and Mr. Gunn crouched at the river's edge and he took a pinch of something from inside his jacket. He held it up and spoke to it, then tossed it into the roily water.

The river was barely below flood stage, brown and opaque and moving at a terrifying pace. When the men slid the canoe into the water, it looked about as sturdy as a dancing slipper, but they steadied it, and the young man swung easily into the back. He gestured to Ephraim and said, "Get in, boy." His voice was low and flat, with a bare trace of British accent.

Ephraim wouldn't budge. The young man was in position with the canoe paddle in his hand. He called out to Ephraim again, but Ephraim could manage only a few steps when the sight of the brown water stopped him.

"Come, boy. Are you deaf? Gideon, is he simple? Climb in, keep low and to the center. She won't rock."

Livy held her breath as Ephraim took another step backward, banging into Mr. Gunn. "Rising Hawk's been on these rivers since he was born," Gunn said, giving Ephraim a push. "This canoe ain't goin' down. Now git."

Ephraim executed a quick left and took off up the bank. Livy started after, but Mr. Gunn was ahead of her and caught him by the ankle before he reached the top. Ephraim fell and slid backward.

Mr. Gunn took him up by the collar and dragged him back to

the canoe. The young man laughed, and Livy turned on him. "It's not funny. You don't understand. Stop it!" The young man looked surprised, then laughed again at her venomous expression.

She flushed, and her voice shook as she repeated, "Stop it!," fully intending to upset the canoe if he mocked her again. He mistook her anger for an onset of tears and stopped.

"Please get in, Ephraim," she whispered, furiously brushing the sand off his jacket, making him wince at the pounding. "God must have spared us for a purpose. Get in and just close your eyes."

Ephraim shook his head. His face was as white as the underbelly of a catfish. There were tears in his eyes, and in front of strangers. Despite herself, Livy felt shamed.

Silently, but firmly, Mr. Gunn took her shoulders and pushed her aside. In a matter of minutes, Eph was tied hand and foot and slung over Mr. Gunn's shoulder. He waded into the water and laid the boy on the bottom of the canoe.

He turned to Livy, prepared, by the look of him, to tie her up as well, but she was already scrambling over the side. Soaked to the knees, she gripped the sides with whitened knuckles, determined to show them that she wouldn't cry, that at least one of them would not be treated like a child. She found herself face to face with the Indian. Despite the shaven head, he was a handsome young man with a good-humored expression in his dark eyes.

He smiled slightly and nodded, acknowledging her small act of courage. The smile broadened as he looked away from her and said, "You should turn around. You will be traveling backward a very long time." Feeling foolish, Livy managed to turn just as the canoe dipped with her master's weight and glided swiftly into the current.

Chapter 3

Livy stood in the yard facing Polly Gunn and feeling tongue-tied and embarrassed. They had traveled in silence until late afternoon, and Mr. Gunn had done little to make the children feel welcome. He had given their names to his wife, burdened Eph with the elm-bark packs, and taken himself off in the direction of the barn. Now Mrs. Gunn's long silence made it obvious to Livy that she and Eph were an imposition.

"Well . . . Deliverance, I suppose you can kill the speckled hen for supper. She's a poor layer and won't be missed. I'm afraid there won't be much to eat tonight, but tomorrow I'll show you how we put up venison. Mr. Gunn brought enough to feed us for a month . . . if we're very sparing of it." Mrs. Gunn paused and looked in the direction of the barn, where the Indian was just disappearing. "Rising Hawk was supposed to be in Grand River. I wonder what made him change his plans?" She spoke more to herself than to Livy.

Livy was staring. Mrs. Gunn was the prettiest girl she had ever seen, and surely far too young to be married to Mr. Gunn. He was handsome, Livy guessed, but looked as if he had been cured in a smokehouse for thirty or forty years.

"The hens are out back. There's an ax by the woodpile, and I'll put water to boil for plucking." She was interrupted by a baby's squawk coming from inside the cabin. "Do you like babies?" For the first time, she smiled at Livy. "Silly question. I've never met a girl who didn't."

"I raised four of them."

"That's not the same as liking them. How many brothers and sisters do you have?"

"None," Livy said, with that prickly, hot feeling she got around the neck whenever grown-ups pried. "I had cousins. I was the eldest, then Eph and the four little girls. They drowned."

Mrs. Gunn's face changed. She had three little ones of her own. Livy saw tears in her eyes. "I'm sorry. How terrible. Then they were the boy's sisters?" Livy nodded. There was an awkward pause, and the baby let out a weak wail. "What happened to your parents?" Mrs. Gunn asked.

"My mother was a war widow when I was born. She wasn't made to birth babies. My aunt and uncle are the only parents I know."

"I see," Mrs. Gunn said quietly. "I lost my parents during the war, too. In prison—typhoid, I think." The baby's wail rose an octave and settled into a newborn's relentless rhythm.

Polly Gunn struck Livy as gently raised. Gentlefolk in prison meant they were either debtors or Tories. Livy stole a look at her face. You couldn't tell a Patriot from a Tory by looks. She hoped Mrs. Gunn's folks had been debtors. There was nothing Uncle John had hated worse than Tories, unless it was Seneca. She wondered if her face betrayed her thoughts.

But Mrs. Gunn only laughed lightly. "You're a bit shy, aren't you? I suppose I am running on a bit, but I haven't seen another woman since Sary Rhodes left poor Ollie. And that was months ago."

Livy ran across the yard, dodging puddles. Sprays of black mud coated her ankles. Homesickness overwhelmed her. She missed Conway with its white clapboard houses and orderly farms. The Gunn homestead was a mess.

Sawdust and logs lay scattered in heaps. A refuse pile of useless scraps and broken pottery sprawled within easy throwing distance of the porch. The yard was muddy, and the big laundry kettle, set on high ground, was an island surrounded by sooty water.

The barn was sturdy, but unpainted and spoiled by a jumble of uneven split-rail fences enclosing a hog and three sheep. The doors were open at each end, bathing the interior with murky light. In the gloom an ox chewed and watched from the shadows. "Livy?" Eph was in the sheepfold, with a pitchfork and a wheelbarrow that held barely a forkful of dung.

"Can you leave that for a minute, Eph?"

He looked up. Even in the dim light she could tell he'd been crying. "I guess he thinks if he keeps me busy I won't have time to be any trouble. He's squatting across the creek, having a pipe with that Indian. They're not working. I'm tired." Eph wiped his nose on his sleeve. "I don't suppose that matters to anyone."

He was grateful that Livy pretended not to notice his tears as she took the fork from him. She easily scooped a pile into the wheelbarrow, then a few more. At least now it looked as if he'd done something. "Thanks," Eph whispered.

"I hate it, too, Eph," Livy blurted. "I hate it. We could work until Judgment Day and never clean it up. How does she stand it?"

"He hasn't even dug a well." Eph sniffed contemptuously. "They take their water from the creek, and the fences aren't even painted."

"That savage is going to sleep in the house!"

"Pa wouldn't approve," Eph said.

"And your mother would have a sit-down spell," Livy said.

"Isn't it odd, Livy? The country's only had this territory since eighty-nine, but he's managed to clear at least thirty acres of trees the other side of the creek."

"Uncle John could have cleared thirty acres in four years, too. More, probably."

"But Mr. Gunn hasn't even bothered to dig a well in all that time."

"Someone cleared it."

Eph kicked a dried clod across the pen. "Well, whoever it was, I'll wager it wasn't him."

Eph caught the fussing hen and deftly wrung her neck, while Livy stood with her back turned. She plugged her ears against the snap and sudden silence until the execution was over and Eph tapped her shoulder.

"Finished," he said, thrusting the hen at her. The warm, twitching body and the dangling head were in her face. She took it gingerly. Back home she had hidden her squeamishness. When she was five, folks were charmed and said it was proof of a warm heart. After that, it was merely weakness. Whoever heard of a farm girl who couldn't kill her own supper? Eph always obliged her, but made her do one of his unpleasant chores as payment. This time Eph didn't mock her. By the time Mrs. Gunn came looking for it, Livy had the chicken plucked and headless and ready for the pot.

Their new master appeared for supper washed, shaved, and dressed like any other farmer in tow shirt and knee breeches. The peculiar odor, merely an Indian concoction to protect skin from bitter weather, was gone, along with the oafish behavior. Livy was puzzled to observe that between Mrs. Wilkes's table and his own, Gideon Gunn's table manners had improved.

The family stood for grace, the children sitting only after the adults had been seated. The master and mistress took either end of the table, with the Indian and the children on benches along the sides. Livy, seated opposite the young man, could not rid her mind of her uncle's war stories, particularly the ones about the Seneca cooking and eating their enemies. Shaken, she dropped her spoon twice, then bumped her head retrieving it. The Indian—Rising Hawk—conversed freely and easily with the master and mistress. But whenever he was unobserved, he stared coldly and steadily at Livy, until she dropped the spoon a third time and fled the table.

After supper Livy and Ephraim fetched the dishwater and cleaned the pewter dishes and small kettle with scouring rush. Then they fetched in water and wood for the morning, swept the floor, and scoured the table board.

Four-year-old Henry wiggled and laughed amiably as Livy washed his grubby feet. But Hannah refused to let Livy touch her.

If Livy came too close, Hannah ran as if from ambush. Livy was mortified. At bedtime Hannah circled the room giving toddler kisses, solemn and open-mouthed, but burst into howls when she caught sight of Livy climbing the ladder to the children's sleeping loft. "She must have thought that girl was gone," Rising Hawk said loudly to Mr. Gunn, trying to be heard over Hannah's wailing. "She wants you to give her back. Babies know about people." When Livy stopped suddenly and looked down, he smiled slyly.

The loft rafters were empty of food stores. Only two stalks of last year's tobacco hung at the far end. A basket of flaxseed was pushed into a corner, waiting for the spring planting. Little Henry was already asleep in his bed in the chimney corner.

Livy lay down on her makeshift pallet of pine boughs, wondering how the Indian would react if she leaned over the railing and spit on him. Her imagination lingered over images of hitting the mark. She followed an imaginary track of spit down his face. It was satisfying and quelled her anger. She listened to the steady murmur of adult voices from below. The heavy scent of tobacco mixed with sumac leaves began to fill the loft. Eph turned over on his pallet to face her.

"There's a row of nearly rotten elm stumps behind the barn," he whispered. "A row deliberately cut, not brought down by a storm."

"Then he's been here longer than the village." Livy did a quick calculation. "Elm takes at least twelve years to rot, so they must have come down in eighty-one, but this is 1793, and the village has only been settled for four years. Nobody lived here when General Sullivan came through."

"Nobody but Seneca," Eph said.

Downstairs Mr. Gunn's voice rose above the Indian's, his words melodic and unrecognizable. Eph lay on his back and closed his eyes. "Mama wouldn't have liked these people, Livy. Pa, neither," he whispered. In a moment he was asleep.

Livy lay awake for an hour, listening to the low voices of the grown-ups still at the fireside. She was terrified she'd hear her name mentioned, and there was no way to shut out the voices. Mr. Gunn talked a long time about his hunting trip. A few times he used Indian words, and she wondered if, somehow, he knew she was listening. Then the Indian said something in his savage tongue, and the missus laughed. Livy moved uneasily at that. Polly Gunn's parents had died in a prison, and now it appeared she talked Seneca, too. Livy curled up on her side and pulled the blanket over her head. There was more to her new mistress than gentle manners and a pretty face.

If only, Livy thought, if only Uncle John hadn't insisted on coming, they'd all be alive and we'd be home. "I want to go home," she whispered into the darkness. "I want to go back to where I belong." She closed her eyes. Down below a bench scraped, and she heard the Indian say good-night.

Later, when the night was fully dark and the only sound was an occasional squirrel padding across the roof above her head, she drifted off and dreamed she was struggling alone in high, rushing water. And everywhere she looked for help, she saw Indians with painted faces.

Chapter 4

Early April was rock-clearing time. Winter's freezing and thawing had brought a new crop of rocks to the surface, and it was Ephraim's job to clear the worst of them away. He pried a rock from the wet soil and squatted to lift it. Mud was lodged under his fingernails and coated his arms to his elbows. His shirtfront was more soil than cloth. Eph pivoted, tossing the rock onto the waist-high pile behind him. Master Gideon had been complaining that it wasn't higher by now. The rock landed with a thud, setting off a minor avalanche. As Eph straightened, he could see the Indian, Rising Hawk, skirting the muddy field about fifty yards to his right. Eph lifted another rock as Rising Hawk passed behind him without a word.

Eph tossed the rock angrily and sat down on the pile. He'd been with the Gunns for two weeks now and had spent half that time clearing the old cornfield. He was sick to death of it. Master had set him to work this morning and gone off with his oldest son, four-year-old Henry, to where and to do what, Eph didn't know. Nobody told him anything, but he was sure it was more interesting than this.

Back home, his father had had his own bondboy for chores like this. Luke came from a family with more children than money and was one of three brothers bound out to neighbors to save his parents the expense of raising them. It was rumored that Luke's father had struck him too often about the head when he was small, and as a result Luke was slow. He had *liked* clearing rocks. It galled Eph now to be in Luke's place.

"Hey," he shouted at the Indian's back. The young man continued skirting the field and didn't respond. When he slipped into the woods, Eph jumped up and followed.

"It is not deep," Rising Hawk said as he stood in the creek, poised over something, his hands open and waiting. "They swim packed together, so they are easy to catch. Use a club if you wish."

Eph crouched on the bank, stripping a willow branch of its leaves. He shook his head. "No thanks," he said. "I'll string 'em for you."

Rising Hawk moved suddenly and, with a scooping motion, sent a large, grayish fish flying through the air. It hit the rocky bank at Eph's feet and lay still a moment, stunned, then came to with a slap of its tail. Eph threaded the branch through its gill, slid it to the center, and laid it on the bank.

"Are you afraid of the water?" Rising Hawk asked, bending forward again.

"No!" Eph protested, then blushed a little, remembering the canoe. "We used to do this at home. I just don't want to be wet and cold all day."

"That girl would do it," Rising Hawk said quietly.

Eph shrugged. "Probably. She can't help herself." He grinned smugly at Rising Hawk and sank to sit cross-legged on the bank. "She ought to calm down."

Rising Hawk was concentrating on the water downstream. "This fish is bony but good. You do expect to eat with us tonight, don't you?"

Eph ignored the hint. "Back home we go after eel in the fall. Just peel 'em off the ledges, like picking berries." He scooted down on his belly on the rocky bank to illustrate. "They're usually right under the rock shelf. Do you do that here?" he asked, propping his chin in his hands.

Rising Hawk nodded wordlessly, then jumped forward with a scooping motion. This one hit Eph full in the face.

Livy set the supper dishes just hard enough so that Polly knew she was angry. Gideon had said very little when Eph wandered in carrying Rising Hawk's catch but sent him right back to the field to make up his lost time. Eph had picked rocks for three solid hours and was so fatigued that his hands trembled. When Livy had questioned him, Eph had been evasive, but muttered something about Rising Hawk asking for help.

"Do you think the weather will hold for planting, Ephraim?" Gideon asked. "If there's no rain, the fields should be dry enough to plant in two days, don't you think?" There was no response from Eph, who sat in disgrace in the chimney corner, smoldering and eating his supper of bread and water apart from the rest. Gideon winked at Rising Hawk and got a snort of laughter in reply.

It's your fault, Livy thought, glaring at Rising Hawk over her plate of fish and dandelion greens. You enticed him away just so you could make him do the work. And you didn't even stick up for him.

Rising Hawk met her eyes suddenly. "What is the matter?" he asked, genuinely puzzled. "Don't you like fish?"

Eph's rock clearing was finally halted by good weather. The fields had dried, and everyone was to begin planting the early corn at first light. As usual, Livy was up an hour before dawn building up the fire to cook samp, the cornmeal mush she'd been making since childhood. Rising Hawk, dozing in his bedroll near the hearth, was in the way and narrowly missed being trampled by Livy as she hurried about. She didn't even try to be quiet.

He opened his eyes and squinted in the weak firelight. She was a dark blur through his eyelashes, flitting around like a fly. She tired him with her constant activity. Even when she sat down, which was rare, she would pull some trifle from her apron pocket and mend it, or unravel it and fashion it into some other trifle. He understood that women, his mother included, admired capable women. But this child was relentless. She set herself so many tasks that her face was always screwed into an unpleasant scowl.

Livy leaned down into the cornmeal barrel, aware that Rising Hawk was awake and watching. She had learned to sense his presence. Like sheep sense a wolf, she thought grimly. It's no wonder

Seneca think up all that devilment to do to Christians. Any man that lazy has nothing better to do. Uncle John had spared them none of the grisly details in his endless retelling of the massacre he had witnessed at Cherry Valley: blood mixed with slushy snow and the American soldiers barricaded in the fort, outnumbered and helpless. It was as real to Livy as if she'd been there herself.

The teasing had started that first evening, when Rising Hawk discovered that all he had to do to set Livy's hands trembling was stare at her. He used this knowledge cruelly. He was sly; neither Gideon nor Polly ever caught him at it. Livy found herself blushing and flustered, dropping things, knocking them over, until even Polly lost patience. Then, when she grew hardened and could no longer be shaken by his cold looks, he made a direct attack. He waited until she was sweeping mud off the steps, came up behind her, and grabbed her single braid of hair. He let out a war cry. Her reaction had been rather more than he expected, and her scratches and an angry lecture from Gideon took most of the fun out of it. But soon, to his delight, he had discovered another torment.

He found that not only did she demand hard work from herself, but she expected everyone to be as driven as she. It infuriated her when he simply watched. Yesterday, for instance, she spent a quarter of an hour coaxing a stubborn cow into the milking stall when one shove from him would have done it. He had never seen her so frustrated.

Livy straightened up. The cornmeal was low. They'd have to find something to barter with at Tyler's store, or go without. She ran her hand through the measure of meal, looking for weevils, and found a pebble. She dropped it onto the hearth and glanced at Rising Hawk, pretending to sleep not three feet away. It would serve him right if that pebble fell into his breakfast. A cracked tooth provided a lifetime of pain and would pay him back for his tricks and his sneaking around. Trouble was, they all knew how careful she was about such things. She'd get caught and be forced to apologize to an Indian. It was bad enough she had to feed one all the time.

"But he's a warrior," Polly said when Livy complained to her later that morning. The whole family, with the baby in a cradle board, were in the field. Rising Hawk had seen them off, then disappeared into the woods. "Seneca women do the farming and take pride in it. Those ladies would laugh themselves silly if they saw Rising Hawk planting corn, and he'd never hear the end of it. Why, he's no more likely to take up farming than Gideon would be to leave off being head of this family. Besides, he's not as lazy as you think. You should go on a deer hunt sometime, Livy. Spend your whole day toting a ten-pound Kentucky rifle in the snow and the cold and see how you feel when it's over."

Chapter 5

They were planting their second acre when Ephraim took sick. It was a new field, and the soil was so loose that they didn't need the plow. The day before, Master Gideon, then Ephraim, had run the harrow over the field to open it up. Now they planted hills, four kernels to each. In every seventh hill, when the weather warmed, they would also plant beans and squash. Gideon said it was the Seneca way and worked well, shading out weeds and providing big yields.

Nobody thought it peculiar that Ephraim should lag behind. He was no more enthusiastic about planting than he had been about rock clearing, and they expected nothing better. So when he did go down, face first, into a hill he had just planted, he lay there several minutes before the others, who were well ahead of him, even noticed.

Polly reached him first. Henry was close behind, morbid curiosity moving his small feet. Polly heard him coming and turned quickly to intercept him.

"Livy," she called, her sharp tone betraying her fears. "Keep the children away!" Livy shepherded Henry off, her face as pinched as Ephraim's.

Polly rolled him over and brushed the dirt from his face. He moaned when her fingers touched him, and tried to roll back.

"Lie still," she ordered. She opened his shirt, pulled his breeches low on his belly, looking for telltale redness, and was feeling for swelling at his neck when Gideon scooped him up.

"No rash," she said. "But he's hot. Likely it's settler's fever. His appetite has been very poor. I wondered at it."

"It's more likely bile," Gideon grumbled. "This is going to put us behind." He turned toward the cabin.

Livy panicked when she saw Eph's arm swing lifelessly at the movement. She dropped Henry's hand and sprinted after, passing Gideon easily.

Rising Hawk was seated on the steps, stringing a small bow for Ephraim. He watched the girl running across the yard and moved aside slightly to avoid a collision as she bounded up the steps and through the door. She was fast for a short-legged woman.

Inside she scurried up the ladder, pushed some bedding over the railing, then scurried back down to arrange it by the hearth. Rising Hawk watched her through the open door, framed as if she were a picture in a book. She had a real capacity for hysteria. It wasn't a quality he admired. Nonetheless, she ran well under its influence.

Livy watched the dark hand with the earthenware cup come closer. She squeezed her lips shut and turned her head on the pillow.

"Drink it. Ephraim drinks everything I give him and he's nearly better."

"It's devil's brew."

"You see?" Rising Hawk spoke to someone behind him. "This morning she wouldn't even take water from my hand. She called me a savage . . . again. Fever has loosened her tongue. When I agreed to do this for Polly, you promised she would be docile. I usually like children, but I can't stand to be in the same room with this one."

"I know. I'm sorry, Rising Hawk, but we're planting short-handed. Polly's worn out with the baby. Just give us a few more days. A week."

Livy turned fitfully on her pallet. "I feel sick."

"You're sick because you won't drink Rising Hawk's tea." Master Gideon seemed to be hollering again. Lately everyone shouted when they spoke and stomped when they walked, and the baby bellowed with the voice of two babies. "Stop being so pigheaded. This will bring your fever down and you'll get better. You drink this right now, or I'll throw you in the creek and hold your head under until you do."

"Can't . . ."

Gideon grabbed the cup, pinched her nose, and when she had to open her mouth to breath, forced her to swallow. He did it twice more before letting go. She shuddered and looked around for a place to spit. Her eyes lit on Gideon's moccasins, and he stepped back.

"I suppose that's enough for now, but no more nonsense, Livy." He handed the cup back to Rising Hawk. "She won't give you any more trouble."

Rising Hawk took the cup with a skeptical glance at Livy. He wasn't convinced. She was rolled into a tight, angry ball at their feet, like a possum. Possums could be nasty little animals when they were cornered.

A fly was crawling up Livy's blanket. It stopped inches from her nose to adjust its wings and pass feathery legs over its eyes. She felt dizzy watching the obsessive fluttering. Suddenly she was over-whelmed with the smell of codfish on the boil. She swallowed and swallowed again. "Outside," she wailed.

Rising Hawk helped her up, holding her at arm's length. "Two more days, then no more," he said, and hurried her out the door.

It was dark when Livy woke again. She'd dreamed that Aunt Mary was hanging bundles of lavender and rosemary around her bed. She was bitterly disappointed to see Rising Hawk, on his knees at the hearth, lighting a twist of sweetgrass. He sat down and waved the smoking brand over her.

He was surprised to see her eyes open, watching him. She looked as if she were going to commence a funeral lament. "Why are you so sad? The birds welcome you in the morning, too, the same for us all."

"I want to go home."

"Ah, " he said. He was silent a moment, watching the sweet-grass smoke. "This is your home now."

"No," she said, drawing a ragged breath, "it isn't."

"In time, you will learn to be content," Rising Hawk said. "Meanwhile, I have thought about your misfortunes and"—he paused dramatically—"have decided I should overlook your bad manners."

She was speechless for a moment. Her fever rose. "My manners are much better than yours," she retorted.

"Really? I was taught very young not to wear my angry thoughts on my face. You have given me nothing but angry looks since you came here. You should learn . . . There is a good word Polly uses for this; let me think." He frowned, one hand raised to his ear as if to catch the memory of its sound. "Decorum," he said finally.

Livy scowled and realized too late that she was wearing her thoughts on her face again. "At least I don't go around scaring folks to death. Folks who never did you any harm." She spoke with a self-pitying whine. "You've picked on me at every opportunity and you've been sneaky about it so Polly and Gideon don't know. Is that what you mean by decorum, being sly?"

"You have always been rude, but lately you have been insulting. You have insulted me many times the past few days. You called me a savage. You said your uncle was a soldier and would kill me if I made you drink any more tea. Then you gave a speech about the great Washington, the Town Destroyer, and how he said the Haudenosaunee were just wolves in men's clothing. You gave that speech *twice.*"

Livy wanted to tell him he was a liar, but her fever had gone up and she began to drift again. If she concentrated, she could lift her body off the bed and float. Rising Hawk's complaints grew fainter and fainter, as if they were being carried off by the wind, or in the beak of a bird. She had a brief, satisfying vision of Rising Hawk being carried off by a giant eagle.

"You are a mighty orator when you are ill, and a singer. You sang many songs that made no sense. You also told how you were named. How your mother died and they took you from her dead body. A good story."

Livy struggled to say it wasn't a good story, it was a tragic story and none of his business, but the words were hard to form, and she forgot she had to say them aloud or he'd pretend not to hear.

"This is a story that was told to me, but I do not tell it as well as they used to." Rising Hawk's voice. A sickening smell of tobacco. Livy turned over, trying to get away from it.

"Turtle was dissatisfied and complained, 'Turtles have no glory. We achieve nothing like the great deeds of the warriors of mankind. We inspire no fearful respect like Bear or Panther. All we do is raise our families and tend to our homes. One cannot spend a lifetime sunning oneself on a log. Surely the Creator expects more from us. I intend to bring honor to the turtles by leading a victorious war party.' The turtle wife refused to supply him with moccasins or food for the perilous journey, hoping to discourage him. But Turtle chose to ignore her wise counsel and set off in his canoe anyway."

Livy opened her eyes. Rising Hawk sat very straight against the hearthstone, his face stern, and it seemed he spoke the words without moving his lips. His hands moved, cutting through the air, demonstrating how slowly, deliberately a turtle would paddle a canoe. His voice rose and fell, and Livy closed her eyes and let herself be drawn in.

The determined turtle went on to recruit a war party of unlikely warriors: a skunk, a rattlesnake, and a possum. Despite their brave words and determination, their war was a dismal failure. In their first and only battle, all but the turtle were quickly dispatched by a trio of angry women. Livy heard Henry and Hannah giggle as Rising Hawk did the women's voices, mimicking Polly's for the fiercest.

Finally, chastened but wiser, the turtle ended his tale: "Perhaps I am not a great warrior, but I am a turtle and can be content with that. After all, the earth and all its beauty rest upon a turtle's back.

That is glory enough." Livy didn't know how he did it, but the turtle was speaking in her voice.

Polly talked Rising Hawk into staying for her sake. Ephraim recovered quickly and in a week he was able to go back to the fields and help Gideon and Polly finish the planting. By then Livy could sit up, and Rising Hawk was able to move outside for most of the day, taking short forays into the woods to relieve his boredom. When he stayed, he lolled on the porch near enough to help if she needed it, but out of sight, so that as long as they were quiet they could enjoy the illusion of being alone. By now they were heartily sick of each other.

The cabin seemed unbearably gloomy and the air outside too cold for convalescing. Livy tried reading her Bible but couldn't concentrate. She sat down at the big loom that took up half of the wall opposite the hearth. Polly was finishing a length of blue cloth that was to be a shirt for Rising Hawk. Livy spent five minutes passing the shuttle back and forth and then was too exhausted to move. She was forced to humble herself.

"Rising Hawk," she said, speaking to the empty doorway, "would you tell me a story, please?"

There was a slight hesitation and then a curt "No."

She flushed red. She would have cut out her tongue rather than ask why.

There was a long pause, then Rising Hawk appeared in the doorway. "Last night Gideon reminded me that the season for those stories is over. Sometimes he is an old woman about these things, but he's probably right. It's not wise to anger the spirits."

"Why does he know so much?"

"In some ways, he is more traditional than our oldest sachems."

"I don't understand."

"He is the eldest. I listen to my elder brother, or I let him think I do. He can be . . . What's the word for it?"

"I have no idea what you're talking about."

"The big nose. You know, telling everyone what to do."

"You don't mean really your brother. He's not an Indian."

"Yes, he is. I thought you knew that. Why else would I be here?" He looked at her face. Her confusion was obvious.

"You are puzzled," he said. "This is a story I can tell. Before the American war, the Haudenosaunee were powerful."

"What's the Haudenosaunee?"

"The Six Nations. The Iroquois Confederacy. Don't interrupt.

"For generations we gathered many people into our nets— Huron, Delaware, many of the southern tribes. They all became a part of us, the People of the Longhouse. Now, long before I was born, six winters before, Gideon was given to my mother. This is how it happened.

"Hunting parties from other nations never passed through our land without permission. But this time a small party of very young men, Miamis, who were inexperienced and stupid, tried to pass through without being noticed. In doing so they caused a dispute and killed one of our people. My father was part of the war party who punished them. They were insignificant fighters, too young. There were no older warriors to keep order and inspire them with courage, and they disgraced themselves.

"It was quickly over. Our warriors killed the others but took one Miami captive. Then they found Gideon hiding behind a rock, all curled up like a sleeping squirrel. He had been mistreated, was naked, half-starved, and completely silent. The Miami captive swore they had rescued him, that he had been lost and would have died without them. No one ever knew where he came from. My father felt sorry for him, so he carried him all the way home on his back. Because he carried him, and the Miami captive satisfied the family who had been wronged, my father kept Gideon."

"How did he learn English, then?" Livy asked. "If he was that young and grew up in your family, how could he remember how to speak it?"

"He didn't. Gideon grew up speaking our language. He only learned English because Anglican missionaries saved him when he was nearly killed in the American war. He was up north near the border. Mohawks took him to the mission in Canada because he was too far from home to be carried back. They thought he was going to die anyway, and didn't want to make his journey any harder.

"He didn't die. He spent four winters there, in a school for girls. He was the only boy because Father Clairemont decided to tame him and make him white. Gideon was too sick to argue. For a while he thought he was a captive because Father Clairemont kept him by his side during the day and locked him in at night. Finally he got used to everything, except their shoes. He refused to wear them, but Father insisted, so he threw them in the river rapids. When Father asked him where his shoes were, Gideon told him and was beaten for it. Gideon says he learned English and lying at the same time.

"Still, he thought it was useful to know, especially after the war, when the Americans came and had to be talked to if we were to make treaties. He came home then and taught me a little and got the women to let me go to Father Clairemont for a while so I would have to speak it all the time. Father Clairemont gave me an English name as he had my brother. They called me 'Isaac' at the school, but they never tried to give me shoes. Gideon stayed with me. He told me it was to help me learn to read, but really he was there to see Polly. When we came back, she came with us. My mother was very disappointed."

Livy looked uneasy, and Rising Hawk wondered if he had offended her. He knew she had a suspicious nature and often mistrusted people. Ephraim was easy to understand. Like most boys, he was a pest, but as transparent as a pool of water. But Livy . . . sometimes he believed she harbored a dark spirit somewhere inside. It was too bad. A good mind and a dark spirit couldn't live together in the same girl.

Livy was remembering Uncle John's war story about the death of Lieutenant Boyd, about captives tethered to a sapling, on a leash, unable to escape the ring of fire encircling them, slowly roasting to death. Rising Hawk couldn't be more than twenty, so he was practically a baby during the war, but Master Gideon was near thirty. Uncle John said that to the Seneca, a boy of fourteen might be a warrior, if he showed an aptitude for it.

"Rising Hawk, you said Master Gideon was hurt in the War for Independence."

"Yes."

"But what side did he fight on?"

"He didn't fight. He was hunting. The soldiers saw a Seneca warrior, so they shot him. They didn't stop to ask if he had joined a war party."

"But what side was he on?"

"Why, the king's, of course."

Chapter 6

The Indian in the red coat came on a warm night in early June and left with Gideon and Rising Hawk the next morning. Gideon and Rising Hawk knew him and talked Indian with him for a long time. Whatever he said made Gideon's face go angry, then solemn, and he listened hard and said little. After supper he went walking with Polly and the little ones, and when they came back it was Polly who looked solemn and angry.

Livy and Ephraim were left to clean up while Rising Hawk and the strange Indian sat on the porch and talked quietly. The earplugs and nose ring he wore made the Indian's middle-aged features fierce and Livy uneasy.

"He's wearing a British officer's coat, Eph. And his hair isn't like Rising Hawk's, nor his shoes. He came walking in from the west, too."

"Nearly all the nations are west of the Genesee now, Livy. That doesn't mean anything."

"It means he *could* be from Ohio Territory, or one of the British forts. It means he *could* be Shawnee or Miami. Two years ago on the Wabash they destroyed half of General St. Clair's army. We're at war again, Eph. Those folks in Ohio Territory are carrying guns everywhere now."

"Don't fret, Livy. The Haudenosaunee aren't at war."

"Yet," Livy said darkly.

"If it's any comfort to you, they are talking Seneca," Eph said, reaching to put a stack of tea cups on a shelf. "They said something about a creek, *ga-hun-da* or something like that, with another word, a name or something, because they've said them together three or four times. And I think they said the word for 'poison.' Even Rising Hawk looked upset then, and he usually doesn't show things," he added thoughtfully.

"Is Rising Hawk teaching you those words?"

Eph turned red. "He's been showing me how to follow a trail. He's teaching me about the plants and things, too. You needn't look like that, Livy. It's not a crime."

"Your father would be real proud, Eph. You can't even read through a sermon on Sunday, but you manage to learn a heathen tongue."

"It's only a few words . . . "

"Every day I worry about keeping us together, covering up for you when you run off to the woods with that stupid bow of yours."

"It's not stupid."

"I'm endangering my immortal soul with all these near-lies I have to tell, all so you can run off and play Indian. We never have been close, and I don't expect you to actually love me, Eph, but I do think you could show some loyalty."

"But I do love you, Livy," Eph said in a small voice. "Even when you get to nagging on me. It reminds me of Mother."

Livy turned redder than he. "I didn't mean to make you say that."

"You didn't. It's all right."

Gideon and Rising Hawk left after breakfast the next day with the stranger.

"Three weeks," Gideon had told Polly, as they said their farewells on the porch. The other two men stood at a distance in the yard, waiting. Livy walked baby Samuel back and forth in the doorway, rubbing his back gently. "I'll be back for first haying." He touched Polly's cheek and she took his hand, but was silent. The baby pumped his legs and burped. Gideon glanced his way and noticed Eph still sitting at table.

"Stir yourself, boy. You've got to take those sheep to the little falls and get them cleaned up for Ollie. He's coming to shear them this morning." He turned his back, still holding Polly's hand, and Livy heard him whisper, "Just tell him I was called away, Polly. Ollie's not one to ask questions. Ephraim," he said sternly, looking over his shoulder, "if you disobey Polly, I told her to put your bow in the fire. There's three little 'uns to look after; you don't need to make it four."

Eph's "Yes, sir" was mournful. Rising Hawk had given him the bow over a month ago, but they'd been so busy he'd had precious little time to practice. He was feeling especially sorry for himself now, being left behind. Gideon showed little sympathy. "Move," he growled.

"Folks out here sure travel a lot," Livy remarked. She and Polly watched the men until they were out of sight. "And all by foot, too. Back home, at least we'd use a horse and wagon or a sled. Where are they going? Is it far?"

"Friends," Polly said vaguely. "It's far enough. They need Gideon's help with something, and he didn't feel he could refuse. It's just a survey problem. A boundary or something. It's nothing." Hannah came out on the porch holding up a hurt finger. Polly seemed grateful for the distraction, and the subject was dropped.

The time passed quickly. Ephraim made a supreme effort to be good, so good that Livy began to hope he was settling down at last. Ollie Rhodes came, and he and Ephraim managed to shear the sheep and set the portion of the wool to be dyed to soaking. Ollie was a little fellow about Rising Hawk's age. He was pleasant to everyone and quick about his work, but had nothing to say. About a week after the shearing, he came back to visit—"court," Polly said to Livy, making her blush. He hung about as Livy spun wool and lent her a hand with her chores, but they were distinctly uncomfortable with each other. "Too much alike," Polly said that night. "He needs a talkative woman, and you need a livelier man."

"I don't need any man," Livy said sharply. "They're just a lot of extra work for nothing, if you ask me."

Polly laughed. "You'll change your mind when you're older, Livy."

Livy stood up, and the fire cast her shadow unnaturally large on the wall opposite. "I'm old already. Aunt Mary said I was born old. I won't change, missus, especially about that."

She sounded definite and smug, Polly thought, but forced herself to smile.

Gideon and Rising Hawk had been gone three weeks and were expected back any day. That morning, Hannah had been fretful and troublesome. Polly hesitated to leave her. But the strawberries were ripe, and Livy needed to know the way to the little meadow hidden in the woods. Eph was left at home with Hannah while Polly, with baby Samuel on her back, and Henry and Livy, carrying berry baskets, set off.

It was one of those perfect summer days, with warm sun and a slight breeze carrying the scent of pine. Livy could also detect the odor of ham wafting up from her feet. Polly had made Henry apply a thin coating of pig lard to all their shoes. "It's the one thing sure to scare off a rattler," Polly said matter-of-factly, as Livy paled. "Berry patches and snakes are a natural combination, but pigs go after snakes, and they know it. One whiff of pig and they're gone. Gideon showed me. I was afraid to go berry picking for two years after that, but I've never seen even a garter snake around when I'm wearing pig."

"I like garter snakes," Henry said, with an exuberant hop and a skip. "They stink something awful when you pick them up, but I like the way they feel when they curl on your arm. Did a snake ever curl on your arm, Livy?"

"No, not that I recall, Henry. Should I try it sometime?"

Henry nodded eagerly and skipped ahead.

It still seems like a dream, Livy thought. Rattlesnakes and pig grease and strange Indians from out of nowhere in the night.

"Look!" Henry stopped dead and pointed to the ground at his feet. A bright green grass snake, evidently unacquainted with pigs, crossed the path right in front of him, as smooth as a ribbon of water.

They filled their baskets and were back in less than two hours. Polly heard Hannah's wails and the panic behind them before either Livy or Henry. She sprinted ahead so fast that Henry panicked, too, and ran to catch up, crying, "Maaamaa!" in tones nearly as pathetic.

Hannah was tethered to the white pine, tangled in rope nearly to her neck. Trying to break free, she'd somehow managed to hogtie herself and was sitting on the ground about ten inches from the trunk. Her tow shirt was caught up over her belly, so her naked backside was nesting in pine needles. When she caught sight of her mother, she opened her mouth in a cry so tremendous and breathless that no sound came out for three long seconds. While Polly held the shaking toddler, Livy untangled knots. She had barely found the end of the rope when Gideon and Rising Hawk dragged into view, exhausted from their long journey.

Gideon had sense enough to control himself and greeted Hannah with a caress and soothing words, but the sudden reappearance of Papa was reason for more howls. When Eph came tearing in, expecting to find Hannah being mauled by a panther, the entire family turned and, with the exception of Rising Hawk, began raging at once.

When the worst of it had passed, Eph stammered, "Is . . . is she all right? I swear I was only gone a moment. I went to check on my traps."

Gideon's voice was deadly. "You left my child tied up while you went to check on *rabbit* traps?"

Eph hadn't intended to be caught, let alone hurt little Hannah. He couldn't speak, and Gideon didn't seem to expect an answer anyway, because he seized Eph by the collar and dragged him, too, stunned to resist, down to the creek. Hardly breaking stride, he forced Eph to his belly at the edge of a deep pool and pushed his head and shoulders underwater. Eph's arms shot up, flailing around, trying to break Gideon's hold.

For a moment Livy was too shocked to react. Another moment passed, and then Eph's legs started to kick as he tried to heave himself out of the water. "He won't let him up. He's drowning!" She was halfway across the yard before Rising Hawk caught her.

"He won't let him drown," he said, sidestepping her frantic kicks. "It is cowardly to hit a child, but sometimes you have to get their attention. It is all right," he said gently, as she continued to struggle. "It is our way. Gideon won't really hurt him."

Livy was breathing hard and glowered up at him. She yanked her wrists suddenly, but he held on, surprised by her power. "I will let you go when it's over. This is between them. You know the boy deserves it."

Gideon finally let Eph surface. He coughed and gulped for air on his hands and knees, while Gideon lectured him sternly.

Rising Hawk let go, and he was surprised that Livy didn't run immediately to Eph. She moved a few feet away, but just stood there. She looked across the yard at Eph. He was sitting cross-legged on the bank, staring and listening to Gideon's stream of angry words. Timidly, Eph glanced her way. For a moment his expression broke her resolve. Then, with a supreme effort of will, she frowned and turned her back. "I hope it sticks this time," she said quietly. "Uncle John never whipped him. But even he would have punished him for this." She walked back to Polly and the children.

When Gideon finally dismissed Eph, it was Rising Hawk he went to.

Chapter 7

Livy's sunbonnet hid her face from the hot July sun as she bent to the dried flax stalks. With both hands, she uprooted a handful of stalks, then dropped them to the ground. There were fifty hard, dusty steps to complete before they'd have fiber to spin into thread, and this was the first. Singing softly to herself, she moved slowly but steadily into the acre of flax, her body swaying in a continuous, rocking motion as she worked. Every task had its own rhythm. She surrendered to it, letting her mind drift.

"Where's Ephraim?" Livy jumped at the sound of Gideon's voice approaching. Rising Hawk's claiming Gideon as his brother and the sudden appearance of that Indian in the night had aroused her suspicions. Uncle John had always helped a neighbor in need, but Livy doubted he would have left a young wife and five children alone for three weeks to do it.

"He was supposed to be weeding corn with you and Henry," she said warily. Why did Gideon always expect her to keep track of Ephraim? That morning she and Polly had made plum preserves, carded wool, spun, ironed, boiled an onion-skin dye for stockings for Hannah, finished a cheese basket, woven ribbons and hair laces on the little tape loom, and spun some harness twine. It annoyed her that he never seemed to regard their constant choring as real work.

Gideon's sun-darkened face grew darker. "I sent him over to help you an hour ago."

"He's not here," she muttered sullenly. She guessed Eph was probably shooting chickadees. Rising Hawk said it was the traditional first target for a boy. Eph, being old for a beginner, was determined to work himself up to squirrels before the week was out.

"Well damn it! He's gone off hunting again. I'll have to take that bow away from him. When you see him, you tell him for me he's to stay in this field until the last stalk's pulled. I don't care if he's at it all night. Do you hear?"

As soon as Gideon was out of sight, Livy ran for the woods to warn Eph. Gideon was a mild-tempered man, but he was losing his patience with Eph. The dunking had been effective for only about a week.

Livy knew his usual paths, but got no answer to her calls and saw no sign of him. Moving quickly, she soon found herself too far west, in tangled brush she had no recollection of. Defeated, she turned north, knowing she could find the creek and easily follow it home. The brush ended on a bluff overlooking the creek. It was a pleasant spot where the river widened in a curve, and the far bank was low and open and sunny. A nice, level field, she thought to herself. But you couldn't plant an early crop of anything there. It floods in the spring. Then she saw the longhouse, only twenty feet to her left, facing west.

The yard surrounding it was overgrown with saplings and grapevines. There were no paths or open spaces. It was desolate. The ruins of another longhouse lay farther back in the trees, the roof collapsed in, vines strangling two young maple trees growing up through the center. Her curiosity overcame caution. She peeked into the doorway of the intact house. The door at the other end was hanging on strap hinges, letting in enough light to show a dim interior. She just had time to make out a long row of broad shelves lining both walls, when she noticed that a grapevine winding its way up the exterior wall had been cut off. The roof where it had once embedded itself had been repaired with a new section of elm bark. It was still oozing sap at the edges. Someone had fixed it. Just before the panic set in, she thought, They're here. The Seneca have come back.

She tumbled down the bluff in her haste, skidding into the

water with her skirts riding up. Frantically cursing and fumbling at the wet tangle, she scrambled to her feet and ran. Dodging low branches and poison ivy vines, she followed the bank downstream as far as she could, then took to the middle of the creek when the banks became impassable. She fell twice. When the hay meadow came in sight, she waded heavily to shore and held her breath and listened. Nothing, except the sound of water streaming from her skirt and the constant rush of the creek.

No one had followed her. The forest behind and the fields in front were full of the drone of summer insects and the far-off caw of crows. The homestead lay before her, slumbering in the heat. Blushing, she realized she had spooked herself, like a colt shying from the flutter of white on a clothesline. She twisted her skirt angrily. "It's probably just Rising Hawk fixing up a place for himself," she muttered. "Thank goodness he and Gideon weren't here to see me come tearing in like the whole Seneca nation was at my heels."

She strolled across the yard slowly to catch her breath and collect herself. Polly had probably fallen asleep with the children, and Gideon was still in the fields. She stopped at the clothesline, a length of harness twine she had woven herself, and stripped to her small clothes. She hung up her dress and overgown and spread them to catch the sun. Despite the heat, she shivered as she pushed open the cabin door.

A roomful of dark heads turned to look as she did.

Chapter 8

Eph slipped unnoticed through the cabin door only moments behind Gideon, who, lucky for Eph, was in the midst of a family reunion. Livy was just emerging from the loft in dry clothes, her cheeks still tinged with embarrassment at being seen half dressed.

Surrounding Gideon were four men, their four near-naked little sons, and an older couple, who were obviously Gideon's parents. His father, Cold Keeper, was middle-aged, upright, and vigorous; his mother, Buffalo Creek Woman, energetic and cheerful. It was clear that she doted on Gideon. He returned their affection boisterously. Livy and Eph exchanged looks. Then Buffalo Creek Woman and Cold Keeper presented Polly with gifts for the baby.

While more gifts were passed around, Henry sat next to the old man, fingering the carved wooden spoon hanging from his sash. Cold Keeper touched Henry's shoulder lightly and, pointing to the spoon, said, "*Ahdoquasa.*"

"*Ahdoquasa,*" Henry repeated, running his finger across the figure of a standing heron. Cold Keeper looked pleased.

Livy found it difficult to imagine his kindly features hidden behind black and red paint as he left his village to exact bloody vengeance. It was even harder to imagine Master Gideon small enough to be carried on his back.

Buffalo Creek Woman was dressing the baby in one of the little robes she had made for him, exclaiming at his baby perfection over and over. In true grandmother fashion, over Polly's demure objections, she presented a small deerskin bag of maple sugar to Henry and Hannah. They promptly ate it, spoiling their supper.

The men had gone outside to eat. They were settled comfortably on the ground, occasional laughter punctuating murmurs of quiet conversation. Livy and Ephraim helped Polly and Buffalo Creek Woman serve them dinner. The four boys and Henry and Hannah were crammed onto the porch, solemnly trying to communicate.

Livy and Eph were sent inside to mind the kettle. Livy dropped a handful of greens into the stew and watched Eph stir them in.

"They came all that distance just to see a baby?" she whispered.

"For heaven's sake, they're not a war party. Nothing's going on. Just because Polly's folks were Tories and Gideon lived at that school in Canada doesn't make them dangerous."

"What if he's a British agent, Eph?"

"Don't be ridiculous, Livy. That's a harebrained, womanish idea."

"Why?" she said angrily. "It's your pa said there were plenty of them making trouble out here. He said those British in Upper Canada keep telling the western tribes the king will come to their aid if they war with the Americans."

"Gideon lives right in the middle of Americans. What would he have to gain by starting a war in his own backyard?"

"I don't know, Eph. All I know is what Uncle John said. Upper Canada wants Indian territory sitting between it and America. A strip below Lake Ontario and Lake Erie. If Gideon helps them, maybe the British will give him land as a reward. Rising Hawk's probably in on it, too. He's always traveling over to Canada to the nations at Grand River. Couldn't he be carrying messages to the British garrisons there?"

"Rising Hawk's not a sneak, Livy. Besides, he could never keep big secrets. He'd turn them into stories and blab to everyone."

"I tell you, Gideon's hiding something. Why else would he play the fool for people like the Wilkeses? He pretends he can't read or write in the village, then our first Sunday here he reads the Bible and gives his own little sermon. I think he's scared of something."

"Gideon's not afraid of anything."

"He'd be afraid of Patriots like your pa."

"Why?"

"Because they'd hang him for a traitor."

The sun was up when Rising Hawk rode in, balanced awkwardly on Ollie Rhodes's bay mare. Livy put down her knitting to hold the horse and laughed to see him sliding down so gingerly. Livy had been accustomed to going about with her aunt in a pony cart, but out here the narrow forest trails and lack of roads rendered horses impractical. Most farmers still preferred oxen. Rising Hawk was used to going long distances on foot and could handle a canoe in most waters, but he had a deep suspicion of horses.

Polly had sent for the mare to transport some provisions from a mill near the village. Although it had only been a week, the unexpected company was straining her larder, and she wanted a bag of wheat flour and one of rye.

Ephraim was already bent over the rippling comb in the flax field. He and Master Gideon were pulling the slender stalks through the teeth to separate the seeds. They had an acre to process, and the trip to Deane's mill and back would take a day. So Livy found herself sitting astride Jemmy's bare back, her legs being rubbed raw against the four sacks stuffed with grain draped in front and behind her.

Rising Hawk led the horse along a narrow forest track. In some places the low-lying branches were so thickly twined that Livy had to lie flat against Jemmy's neck. The heat was sweltering, and the horseflies plagued the mare around the ears. To avoid being bucked off, Livy cut a leafy switch and fanned Jemmy all the way to the mill.

The mill yard was busy when they arrived. Several farmers were loading sacks into two-wheel oxcarts. It had been a good year for wheat. The quality and quantity being grown in the region were already a source of pride in the state.

Rising Hawk held Jemmy just long enough for Livy to dismount, then wandered off in search of some shade.

Livy led Jemmy to the grain hoist and held her as a young mill hand slipped a rope harness around a bag of wheat. He looked over at Rising Hawk, settled fifteen feet away, comfortably slouched against the massive trunk of a sycamore.

"He might lend you a hand," he said, fastening the grain hoist's iron hook to the harness. "Haul away," he shouted.

Up on the second floor of the mill, an unseen helper pulled. The windlass gathered the pulley rope, and the sack lifted off Jemmy. It went up and through a window to the grain hopper. The bag would be emptied into the hopper, fed to the grindstones, then sifted and bagged at the meal bin below.

"There's no need," Livy said quietly. "I can manage the mare better than he can."

A farmer loading a cart nearby spoke in a voice loud enough for Rising Hawk to hear. "Those heathen make their women do everything. Lazy dogs." The man's wife sat in the cart, regarding Livy with sympathetic eyes. Red-faced, Livy turned and began rubbing Jemmy's sweaty neck.

"Do you belong to him?" the mill hand asked abruptly, pointing at Rising Hawk. Livy could feel the man's tension, coiled around them like a snake.

She shook her head, frightened by his intensity. "No. He's my guide."

"I'm pleased to hear it," he said, more to the farmer than to her. "I thought maybe the government was giving bondmaids to savages now."

The farmer shook his head in disgust. "Wouldn't surprise me. The government coddles them fair enough. They took up arms against us for the British and lost. Now we pay 'em for land should have been forfeit."

The mill hand nodded in agreement as he fastened a rope harness around the second bag of wheat. He lowered his voice. "What I want to know is, what's the point of buying their land if it don't keep those vermin away from decent white folks?"

There was no answer from the farmer. He had motioned to the young fool to keep quiet. The mill hand looked up to see Rising Hawk standing at Livy's side.

"Ah, well," the boy said, "he don't understand. None of these Seneca know any English. Too stuck up or too stupid to learn it; right, chief?"

Rising Hawk laid his hands against the young man's chest in the traditional Seneca greeting. "*Seegwah*," he said solemnly.

"See?" the mill hand said with a smirk. "He don't know nothing."

Rising Hawk dropped his hands. He hoped the oaf would use his greeting on the next Seneca warrior he met. *Seegwah*, roughly translated, meant, "Get away from me, dog."

They were quiet on the trip back. Livy was reluctant to admit it, but the men at the mill had given voice to some of her own thoughts. Hearing them said out loud like that made her feel ashamed. Rising Hawk exasperated her with his laziness sometimes, but that was between them. Those men didn't know Rising Hawk. It was unfair.

"You understand, don't you, that a child learns nothing unless it does things for itself?" Rising Hawk said suddenly, breaking the quiet, making her start.

"Yes, of course."

Rising Hawk made a sound halfway between a grunt and curse. "So we agree. Good. Now that you know the way, you can go alone next time. I know you are able, even if those fools at the mill imagine you are not. They must think you as slow-witted as them. They have no respect at all for a woman's power." He glanced back at Livy, gauging her response. She stifled the urge to smile and met his gaze solemnly.

She looked away and rolled her eyes a little. Rising Hawk certainly believed in some strange notions. Who could he be thinking of? Surely not his mother. She deferred to the men, seeing to everyone's comfort but her own. And Polly was at the beck and call of children day and night, choring every minute. Even Mrs. Wilkes, for all her meddling and powerful air, never had the last word in anything.

Livy leaned forward, switching at a large-as-her-thumb deerfly that had settled between Jemmy's ears. She wished Aunt Mary were here with her disapproval and thin laugh to agree with her.

Rising Hawk's idea of "a woman's power" sounded like witchery. Another example of his heathen imaginings. It was odd that any man could profess a notion like that without joking about it. But he had been perfectly serious and he obviously assumed that she agreed with him because, of course, she understood her own powers.

Nevertheless, it was pleasing to fancy that she possessed mysterious powers simply by being female. Even if she knew better, it was pleasing.

Chapter 9

Buffalo Creek Woman spent several afternoons by Livy's side at the loom, learning to use the shuttle. Polly had a small bag of last year's flax fibers, hackled and ready for spinning, so Livy also showed Buffalo Creek Woman how to wet her fingers and feel the twist as the little flax wheel spun the fibers into thread and onto the bobbins. Buffalo Creek Woman was an adept and enthusiastic pupil. At the end of the last lesson, she was so pleased that she gave Livy a needle book of dark blue trade material with a tree embroidered on the cover.

At supper that evening, Buffalo Creek Woman sat next to Livy, petting and praising her, forcing Master Gideon to put down his food to translate.

"She says that we are fortunate to have hired such a skilled child. She says that among the Seneca at Jenuchshadego you would be a very strong woman and command a great deal of respect for your abilities. Jenuchshadego is their town," he explained.

Livy blushed. "Please tell her thank you, but tell her any woman can do this."

"She says your modesty indicates a good mind and pleasant disposition."

"What should I say?"

"Nothing. I'll take care of it." He turned to Buffalo Creek Woman and said in Seneca, "Mother, I would like to eat in peace. I know what you're thinking, and I don't like this idea. Harvest season is coming up. We need her. Maybe in the winter, but not now."

To Livy's relief, the conversation ended abruptly.

Following supper, Buffalo Creek Woman went after Master Gideon again, talking a blue streak. He crossed from one side of the porch to the other, as if he were being plagued by skeeters. She followed him, still talking. His pleasant smile faded under her onslaught of words. When he stepped off the porch to escape to the barn, Buffalo Creek Woman trailed behind him. They disappeared inside, and Livy wondered where she had acquired her idea that Indian women were docile. Her aunt would never have dared to badger her uncle in that way.

Polly sat in the rocker, nursing Samuel. Seeing her husband bested, she couldn't help but smile. She gently pressed the tip of her finger into the corner of the baby's mouth, releasing his puckered lips. A thin, bluish stream ran down his cheek. Wordlessly, she handed him to Livy when Buffalo Creek Woman emerged and crossed the yard. The older woman seemed to be in a hurry as she put a hand on Polly's shoulder and ushered her toward the barn.

In the bedroom, behind the chimney, Livy stood over Samuel's cradle, listening. She hadn't meant to eavesdrop, but they had entered so quickly and been in the midst of a conversation so intense that she had frozen when she realized it was about her.

"It will only be for a month. I'll fetch her as soon as first corn harvest is done."

"But she's terrified of your relatives."

Gideon laughed derisively. "My mother's annoying, not dangerous. Livy's not afraid of her."

"But Livy's with us here. She'll be alone in their village. Besides, the houses are smoky and crowded, and they have fleas and lice. You know how fastidious she is."

"It's summertime, Polly; we have fleas, too."

"No one speaks English."

"Unless Peter Crouse is there. He was adopted by the Seneca nearly full growed. His English is better than mine."

"And if he's not there?"

"Rising Hawk can go along. He'll look after her."

"Who will harvest in her place? We have beans to start in a week, and early corn after that."

"John Gage."

"If he's not drunk in Rochester again. He's not reliable."

There was a long silence. Livy looked toward the window, devoid of its usual oiled paper and covered for the summer with a bit of gauze. She measured the distance between floor and sill with her eyes.

Finally Gideon spoke. "She's going." There was another long silence, then Gideon's voice again. "Don't be angry, Polly; it will be good for her. If Livy's to stay with our family, she'd best get used to *all* of it."

"But not so suddenly. She's only now tolerating Rising Hawk, and she's known him for months."

"You coddle Livy too much, Pol."

"Gideon, when you were a child the women had complete charge of you. Not even the sachems would make decisions regarding a child unless they consulted the women first."

"She won't be in any danger. She'll travel to Jenuchshadego and spin. Where's the harm in that?"

"It's a hundred miles," Polly said impatiently. "Anything can happen in a hundred miles."

"But she'll be with my mother and father. She couldn't be safer."

"But why now? Couldn't this wait for a few months?"

"No, it can't. In a few months the Seneca could be at war."

There was a long silence before Polly spoke again. "But you said Cornplanter is opposed, that he believes the western tribes should settle the Ohio border in a treaty council. He said another war would destroy them all."

"He is opposed, but he's just one man, Polly. Some of the young warriors see this as their fight, too. The Seneca don't have kings. He can't act without consent. Neither the British or the Americans seem to understand that."

"But he and his peace delegation were taken prisoner by the western tribes at the Maumee council this spring. Some of the delegates died after they were released. You said Cornplanter believes they were poisoned. Surely the people won't support the western confederacy after that?"

"Some will and some won't. It's a delicate game he's playing, Polly. Cornplanter declared his loyalty for the king a few months ago to pacify the western tribes. In June when Rising Hawk and I went to Buffalo Creek to translate for him, he managed to leave those three American commissioners with the impression the Seneca were neutral."

Livy started. Was that why the Indian had come that night?

"Rising Hawk wouldn't fight, would he, Gideon?"

"God, I hope not. He's a good boy. Just the kind who would get himself killed." Gideon drew a deep breath. He began to pace back and forth. "The nations can't win, Polly. The way I see it, the British want to keep the American trade. No matter what they say now, they won't give the western confederacy much help. That's why Cornplanter wants to prepare for independence now—from the British, the western tribes, the Americans, everybody. Two years ago he asked President Washington for plows for the men, and spinning wheels and looms and teachers for the women. Nothing's happened, and if the western tribes drag the Seneca into another American war, nothing will."

"And it's your mother's idea to have Livy teach them how to spin?"

"Yes, and to weave later on. This may help them be less dependent on the traders when things do fall apart. Once the Americans lose their fear of the Haudenosaunee, treaties will be less lucrative. Cornplanter's looking ahead."

"Father Clairemont always hoped you'd become a missionary."

Gideon stopped with his back to the bedroom doorway. His laugh was short, hard.

"I'm no missionary, but I have to do something."

"But you won't be doing it, Gideon; Livy will. What does she get out of this?"

"She'll get out of harvesting. That should be enough. Try to understand, Polly. When my grandfather was my age, he could walk from the Hudson to Lake Erie and never meet with an enemy. At every village he was assured of a welcome. Now the sad truth is the clans don't even share longhouses anymore, let alone the whole country. It will get worse, Polly. They're still isolated at Jenuchshadego, but whenever the Haudenosaunee are near white settlements, things go bad. They were politicians, diplomats, and warriors, Polly. Now they drink too much and squabble over nothing."

He turned just in time to see Livy's hand sliding from the windowsill, the window gauze flapping as she scrambled away.

Chapter 10

Master Gideon was right behind her. He caught her before she cleared the porch. Taking her by the collar, he dragged her back into the cabin.

"Do you make a habit of listening at doors?"

"No, sir."

"This is the first time, is it?"

"Yes, sir."

"Why didn't you come out?"

"She was surprised, Gideon," Polly said quickly. "You know how shy—"

Gideon stopped her with a gesture. "Polly, my mother took the children to the longhouse. Go fetch them."

"Gideon . . ." For one brief moment, Livy thought Polly was going to defy him, but she didn't. On her way out, she patted Livy's arm and whispered, "Hognose."

Gideon grabbed Livy's arm, hard, and sat her down on the hearth bench. He passed his hand over his mouth, then knelt down so that they were face to face. "I never had you figured for a sneak."

"I'm not. . . ."

"This is dangerous. You can't tell anyone about Buffalo Creek."

"That's why he came that night, that Indian in the red coat?"

"Yes."

"But you just told Polly you were translating so Cornplanter could talk to those Americans. Why would that be dangerous?"

"It's not, in and of itself. But I wasn't working for the Americans, Livy. I've never worked for the Americans, and there are some things I don't want people to know about. If you let something slip to the wrong person, they'll connect me to the Seneca. There might be another war real soon, and the Seneca might be in it. If they are, they won't be siding with the Americans. There was just another council with the western tribes on the Maumee Rapids, and the Shawnee flat out refused to meet with the Americans at Sandusky. Sandusky was supposed to be a peace council."

"How do you know all this?"

Gideon shrugged and said nothing.

"It was your folks brought the news, wasn't it? I told Eph you were a spy. You're a Tory renegade, just like Simon Girty. And he's a murderer. Everyone knows that." Her righteous tone aged her. She looked older, and cocksure of herself.

"I'm not tied to the British or the Americans, Livy. And those stories you've heard only have a penny's worth of truth. Even Girty's not quite as bad as they make out, though he is a mean, ugly, self-serving, drunken son-of-a-pup."

"Why aren't you in Canada?"

"That's pretty much none of your business. I guess Rising Hawk never told you about Oniata, the Dry Hand?"

Livy glared at him.

"You'd best watch out for it. It's a hand that flies around looking for nosy people and pokes their eyes out."

"My father and Uncle John fought Butler and Johnson. They were at Cherry Valley. Were you? They said the Indians had a Seneca war chief. Did you go?"

"No. Would it matter?"

"My father and Uncle John helped bury the bodies afterwards. Women and children, even babies, lying butchered in the snow. The slush was red, mixed with their blood. A hundred or more."

"There were thirty killed, Livy. Your uncle was exaggerating."

"My uncle said that when the scalp's off a body, the mouth hangs all slack in a scream, and he said the Indians killed babies by dashing their brains out."

"He shouldn't have told you that. It's not fitting for a child."

"Neither's getting your brains bashed out." She eyed him defiantly. "It was your Seneca did it."

"And loyalists. They did their share. It wasn't the usual fight. These days Seneca don't usually touch noncombatants, male or female. That kind of blood feud belonged to my grandfather's time. I guess there were scores to settle."

"If Mr. Wilkes knew you were sending me to that Indian town, he'd come take us away and put you in jail."

"Well, he doesn't, so he won't. Be sparing of those threats, Livy. I'm not a bad man, but if I was, you'd be in serious trouble right now."

"I am *not* going to an Indian town."

"What are you afraid of?"

"Being killed," she said, as if he were simpleminded. "I never in my life heard anything good about an Indian."

"That's harsh and ungrateful, Livy. Rising Hawk brought you through the fever."

"That's different. He's practically a Christian."

"Is he? Where did you get that notion?"

"I don't know. He's just different from other Indians."

Gideon laughed. "Exactly how many Indians are you acquainted with? When you were sick, he kept asking me if you had enemies in the village. He was trying to figure out who cast the spell on you. He's no Christian, Livy, but he tended you like you were kin."

"I'm not going."

"Oh yes you are. If I have to tie you to a frame and put you on Rising Hawk's back, you're going."

Livy sprang up, her face red with anger. Gideon stood, too, blocking her exit and out of patience. "Sit down!"

"No! You can holler if you want to and you can make me go if you want to, but you're nothing but a big, dumb hognose snake."

"What?"

"It's because you're not sure. Polly says the more wrong you are, the louder you get. Just like a hognose snake pretending to be a rattler. Polly says as long as I don't spook, you'll . . . "

"I'll what?"

"You'll roll over and play dead."

That got him laughing. He sat down with a snort, and stretched his long legs out in front of him. "I take it you've decided not to spook."

"I've decided not to spook," she said, eyeing him warily, then sat next to him. Gideon smiled at the distance she put between them.

"You know you're going, don't you?"

Livy nodded reluctantly, her face pale and young again.

"Listen, Livy. My mother will spoil you. You'll be overfed wherever you go and you won't be here, putting up with me and harvesting all day in the hot sun. You'll be an honored guest. They'll be celebrating Green Corn Festival soon. You'll like that."

"A pagan festival in a heathen fortress, a hundred miles away from the nearest Christian."

"When you get aholt of something you *never* let loose, do you? The fact is, Livy, in a Haudenosaunee village no one is ever allowed to go hungry or ever gets locked up in jail. The fields are worked in common, so everyone gets fed equal. The absolutely worst thing you can do is be unwilling to share. I never lived near white people as Christian as that."

Polly was back. They heard the children chattering in the yard.

"Don't worry, Livy. I promise you that as an honored guest, you'll be as safe as a baby." He patted her hand. "When you belong to them, Livy, they'll do anything for you."

"But I don't belong to them," she said. "I don't really belong to anybody." And she gave him a look that might have been a challenge or arrogance or desperation.

And that suits you just fine, Gideon thought, as his eyes followed her down the steps and across the yard. She betrayed nothing by her walk. Her way of moving was as impenetrable as the look on her face.

He'd seen that look before. Sometimes on the frontier, in the woods, up in the mountains, the Seneca had come across white men with eyes like that. Solitary creatures with odd habits. Not quite mad, not quite sane, they lived alone, as far away from other human beings as they could get.

Chapter 11

Livy was dreaming about the dog again. Rising Hawk and the others were gone, and the dog blocked her path, snarling, its velvety snout wrinkling delicately as the lips drew back to show white fangs, but she wasn't afraid. She called to it, and it stuck a paw under her blankets and tickled her foot. Its touch was light, but insistent. Annoyed, she kicked at the tickling, unmindful of the teeth.

"Wake up," the dog said in Rising Hawk's voice. "The sun is up."

Livy started awake. Rising Hawk stood over her in the gray morning light. For a moment she wondered if she was still sick, lying in her pallet by the hearth. Then she saw the stick in his hand. He grinned and poked at her foot again, and she remembered. She was on the trail to Jenuchshadego.

"I thought you were the dog," she whispered.

"What dog?"

"The one in my dream. The white one. It talked to me."

Rising Hawk dropped down beside her, his face turned serious suddenly. "Such an animal is sacred to the Creator. You say it spoke to you. What did it say?"

"It told me to get up, in your voice," she said, laughing.

Rising Hawk's frown was a reprimand. "Is that all it said?" he persisted.

"Yes, and you'd all abandoned me," she said, reflecting that, considering how she was slowing them down, they'd be pleased to do just that. Gideon had promised a four-day journey and now, on the fifth morning, they still had a full day's journey ahead of them.

Today they would pass through a swamp and across some rocky mountain ridges. The journey so far had been across river valleys surrounded by gently sloping hills. Today was a daunting prospect, and she was sure her shoes wouldn't hold up well in the swamp.

"White men never come to Jenuchshadego," Rising Hawk had told her with some pride. "Not by themselves or in armies. The Genesee towns are surrounded by white settlers, but not us." He grinned in satisfaction. "Not even the missionaries bother us."

Now he was saying, "This could be a very important dream. But why would a white dog choose *you* as a messenger?" Rising Hawk rested his chin in his hand and frowned. Livy wasn't sure she liked his tone.

"There wasn't any message."

"And it doesn't ask anything of you. This is curious. Perhaps I should tell my mother of your dream. It may mean more to another woman."

"It's just a dream, Rising Hawk. Don't make a fuss. It doesn't mean anything."

There was a flicker of annoyance in his eyes. How could his brother allow such dangerous ignorance to fester in his own home?

"Dreams are more important than anything that happens when you are awake," he insisted. "You can cause yourself great harm if you do not listen. We must find out what it means for you to do. This dream could come from within," he said, indicating his heart, "or it could come from outside of you, from the spirits. To ignore the needs of either can mean sickness for yourself or danger to others, to us." Exasperated by her blank look, he added, "I am really very surprised my brother has not taught you this."

"He keeps a Christian household, and Christians don't hold with such things as dreams," Livy said primly.

"Did you know that the missionaries taught me from that book?"

"I knew all along you had Christian leanings," she said, pleased that Gideon had been wrong about his brother.

Rising Hawk made an abrupt motion with his hand, dismissing her idea. "Is your white God so very difficult that one needs a book to understand him? Actually, I believe the priests wrote it themselves," he confided.

Speechless, Livy watched him roll onto his feet and disappear into the brush. She half expected lightning to strike him. She hated the way he was always thinking about white people and making comparisons and acting superior. Why, she hardly ever gave Indians a second thought. She wriggled out of her blankets and began bundling their bedrolls, squeezing them into the smallest possible packs, tidy and easy to manage. When Rising Hawk emerged from the trees, unscathed, a moment later, she was mildly disappointed.

Rising Hawk wasted no time in acquainting his mother with Livy's dream. She, in turn, conveyed it to her husband, and it spread quickly from there. Livy noticed the company looking at her with new interest. She had suddenly become important to their well-being.

Departure was delayed while the men of the party gathered to discuss the matter. Rising Hawk and Buffalo Creek Woman stood on the fringes, listening. One of the men directed a comment to Buffalo Creek Woman. There followed a prolonged exchange, which ended with her shrugging her shoulders. Then the entire group turned their heads to look at Livy.

Buffalo Creek Woman came to Livy's side, towing Rising Hawk as interpreter. Rising Hawk spoke reluctantly.

"They are concerned that perhaps this is a sign they should not complete the journey today. The animal was blocking your path?"

"Yes, but everyone else had gone on ahead. . . . " Now they will leave me, she thought, in a panic.

Rising Hawk interpreted for his mother. She listened, then said to Livy. "Do you have blood?"

Livy looked blank—at the question and at Rising Hawk's mother speaking English. She glanced at Rising Hawk for help, but he was studying his feet. Buffalo Creek Woman understood her confusion. She said something to Rising Hawk, but he shook his head and continued to stare at the ground. She said something else to him, sharply, but he pretended not to hear. She turned to Livy again.

"Do you have blood?" she repeated. This time she waved her hand in the direction of Livy's lower regions. Livy blushed as she suddenly understood.

Rising Hawk spoke up. "Some feel the dream signifies *orenda* for you alone, and is of no concern to the rest of us."

Livy was too embarrassed to ask what he meant.

"*Orenda* is power; sometimes good, sometimes bad. This dog may be powerful magic for you. A helper when you are in need." Rising Hawk kept his eyes on the ground. "Usually these dreams of power come to you when you come of age." There was an uncomfortable silence. "That is why they need to know . . . about the blood."

Livy raised her eyes to the group. All of them? she thought. Adult men, strangers, discussing my . . . bodily functions as if I were the community brood sow! Frantically she cast about for a suitable explanation. Then she remembered something. She had made Ephraim promise not to mention it to the others. She had been afraid they would make a fuss, or worse, take no notice at all.

"It's not . . . that," she said, blushing furiously. "But it is my birthday today. Do you think that can have something to do with it?"

Rising Hawk thought so. With a look of relief, he conveyed the information to his mother, who nodded vigorously. That settled things. Almost before Rising Hawk was done speaking, the men were hoisting their packs.

Livy ducked behind Buffalo Creek Woman for shelter. It's like they stripped me naked, she thought. And they're so offhand. How would they like it if it was one of them! She felt sick with embarrassment. The worst of it was, Rising Hawk wouldn't leave her alone. He stuck to her side, relentlessly cheerful.

"There is an old story my grandfather told me," he said. "There was a warrior—my grandfather knew him—who dreamed he was captured by our enemies and tortured to death. He was so afraid that it meant he would be captured and killed that he begged his friends and relatives to burn him with fire."

Livy winced and looked to see if he was teasing her. He wasn't.

"So they burned him to make certain that he would not fall into the hands of his enemies as the dream foretold. It worked," Rising Hawk hastened to assure her. "He couldn't walk for six months, but he was never captured. He died in his sleep, years later, an old man with many grandchildren." He grinned happily. "By listening to his dream, he changed his fate, you see?"

"But if the dream wasn't true in the first place, couldn't he have lived to be just as old or older, without hurting himself?"

Rising Hawk shook his head. "Dreams are always true," he said impatiently. "Sometimes we don't understand them. That's not the fault of the spirits." His amazement showed, despite his resolution to be tolerant. This was terrible. If she could not grasp the simplest facts, her mind was a worse tangle than he thought. It was painfully obvious that Gideon's neglect of her education could be dangerous. How could Gideon be so careless and still escape disaster? His *orenda* was strong, but eventually one paid for one's arrogance.

Livy was a puzzle. Once, on a rare occasion when she had put her work aside and gone exploring, she had chanced upon the old longhouses at the creek bend. He had been cutting elm bark on the opposite bank when she hurtled into the water. She pretended to be as dignified as a sachem. What would she say if she knew he had witnessed her fall and had seen her landing straddle-legged as a frog with her skirts bunched to her armpits? He had been hard pressed to stay silent. She had cursed, too. As readily as Gideon. He smiled to himself and glanced sidewise at her. Settlers' women dressed like Seneca women. Plenty of layers outside, virtually nothing underneath.

Livy watched the ground, taking long steps to match his and keep up. She supposed it was too late now to explain about Patience. She had been given to Livy as a fuzzy white puppy and had met a sorry end a year later beneath the runners of a sleigh. Livy glanced at Rising Hawk. He was looking straight ahead, smiling slightly. Livy was sure he was laughing at her. From now on, she would keep her dreams to herself.

She had her first glimpse of the town at dusk. From atop the narrow mountain ridge, she counted forty houses scattered in the valley, in no particular order or pattern. Some of them were ordinary cabins. The rest were small longhouses, resembling upside-down arks in a sea of corn. As they drew nearer the village, Livy could see a group of girls running in some kind of ball game. In the same clearing, some men and boys were lighting a bonfire, the smaller boys skipping and jumping in excitement. Here and there were gatherings of women sitting and talking, some with cradle boards in their laps.

"It's the first time I've seen so many people in one place since we left Massachusetts!" Livy gushed. Rising Hawk smiled indulgently at her outburst. I'm getting as peculiar as the hill folk back home, she thought. Suddenly, there were shouts from her party to the people below, and a small crowd came to greet them as they gained the flats.

Three young women surrounded Buffalo Creek Woman with laughter and talk. They smiled at Livy and called to Rising Hawk, who took Livy's hand and pulled her forward.

"My sisters," he said. "The eldest, Takes Up the Net, then Pretty Girl—she is shy, like you—and Runs Faster." Livy curtsied to each one. She was eager to please and wasn't sure the youngest didn't curtsy back in mockery.

Then, just as exhaustion was beginning to claim her, Rising Hawk took her arm to guide her through the milling crowd and into the doorway of one of the bark houses. Through her fatigue she had an impression of a wide hallway, with two or three fires smoldering at intervals down the length of it. Curious faces, of all ages, looked up at her, or poked out from the many compartments that lined the walls. Children peeked down from the upper shelves. Rising Hawk drew her gently to a seat at the fireside, and she sank down gratefully.

Her bundles were taken, and an old woman, with a face as wrinkled as the bark of a maple, handed her a bowl of fragrant succotash. She managed to overcome her shyness just enough to say "*Hi-ne-a-weh*" as she had been taught. She was aware of Rising Hawk's presence next to her as she ate, slowly, remembering Gideon's suggestion that politeness called for a modest display of appetite. Then she simply fell asleep, still holding the bowl and sitting upright.

The last thing she was conscious of, as someone lifted her and laid her gently on a cushion of cool skins, was the sound of singing and laughter coming from somewhere outside where, as far as she could tell, the Seneca were having a party and the fearsome warriors were husking corn.

Chapter 12

It was blistering hot and nearly noon when Livy woke the next day. For a moment she lay in her sleeping compartment, confused by the deerskin hangings that enclosed her bed. In the murky half-light she could see designs painted on the hangings on three sides. The fourth side was the longhouse wall, with moss stuffed into the chinks. At the foot of the broad bed were bark storage boxes with designs of some material worked into the tops.

She pulled on her shift, gown, and sunbonnet. Then she smoothed down the bed and pulled the curtain aside.

The abandoned longhouse at Gideon's had been as empty of life as a creek bed in August. This one overflowed with activity. At the far end of the longhouse, in the open doorway, some ancient women, too old to spend the day harvesting, were shelling beans. At Livy's end there was the sound of children playing right outside, just past the neatly stacked woodpile at the entry. There was a low fire burning in the nearest fire pit. A large kettle hung suspended over it from a sturdy pole that appeared to be a major supporting beam of the house. Along both walls, curtains were pushed up and draped across the upper bunks, where baskets and bundles were stored. Ropes of braided corn, twists of dried tobacco, and bundles of herbs hung from poles and posts across the ceiling and down the sides of the compartments. More baskets were pushed underneath. Livy's bare feet touched corn-husk mats carpeting the dirt floor.

She left her shoes lying under the bed as she padded toward the door. The hundred miles or so they had traveled, one leg of it through swamp and a great deal of it, at the end, across rocky mountain ridges, had worn the shoes nearly useless. At the entry, she stumbled over a sleeping dog and a smiling puppy with a thumping tail, who rose and followed her amiably into the sunlight.

Rising Hawk was sprawled in the shade of a maple tree, watching three naked children busily decorating another puppy in corn husks and enclosing it in a fence made of kindling. Rising Hawk himself had shed most of his clothes except for a breechcloth and moccasins, and Livy felt uncomfortable as she sat beside him, her linsey-woolsey gown already clinging to her back. The children descended on the new puppy trailing at Livy's heels and imprisoned it in the enclosure as well.

"My mother and sisters are in the fields somewhere. My mother has decided you are a guest and must not work. I thought maybe you could stay alone with the old women, but she wants me to talk for you." He stomped a heel into the dirt like an impatient colt tied to a tree. "Most of the young men are hunting bear and deer for the Green Corn Festival. This would be easier if you were a boy," he said sullenly.

"But you told Gideon you wouldn't mind looking out for me."

"Well, of course, I had to be polite. How could I refuse him?"

"You promised, Rising Hawk. I just walked a hundred miles to get here."

"Yes, and I looked after you the whole way. Now you are safe. Be reasonable, Livy. What am I to do with you?"

"You needn't do anything," she said angrily. "I can look after myself."

"Of course." He seemed relieved. "That is just what I said. You are very reasonable." It was his new word. He stressed every syllable, like a spelling bee contestant. "Have you eaten?" he asked with a smile.

"Not hungry."

Ignoring her anger, he jumped to his feet and disappeared into the longhouse. The three children—boys, Livy noted with some embarrassment—lifted a puppy from the enclosure and dumped it uceremoniously into her lap. Then they squatted next to her and began to explain the game, all chattering at once. The smallest pressed up next to Livy and rubbed gently at the side of her face. She laughed and rubbed his. He seemed surprised when he examined his fingers.

Rising Hawk reappeared carrying a large piece of some kind of bread and a drinking gourd. He had pulled on a long, calico shirt that fell nearly to his knees. "We are very isolated here," he said, nodding toward the boy. "He's never seen a white woman. Here," he said, handing her the bread.

The puppy lifted his nose curiously, but made no attempt to grab the food. Livy took a bite. It was like a cake, made of cornmeal, but full of maple sugar and hickory nuts. She took another greedy bite before offering some to the watching children. They smiled shyly and shook their heads. One of them retrieved the puppy, who stared longingly at the bread as he was lowered back into his prison.

An old woman came shuffling around the corner of the longhouse. She had an enormous bundle of wood laid across her back and secured with a strap that looped around her forehead for balance. She swung the burden from her back onto the already large pile just inside the entrance. Livy noticed a ridge from the strap that appeared to be permanent, crossing her forehead. She scrambled to her feet to curtsy, and greeted the old woman as she had heard Rising Hawk greet the mill hand. "*Seegwah*," she said.

The next instant, the burden strap landed on her shoulder with a painful slap. The old woman was raising her hand for a second blow when Rising Hawk stepped between them. He spoke rapidly and took the strap from her hand.

The old woman listened, scowling. Then she answered and seemed to scold him thoroughly, before turning to Livy and delivering an avalanche of words.

Rising Hawk translated. "She says she allowed you to sleep this morning because you were obviously exhausted from your journey, but that she won't allow such laziness again. If you expect to eat with the rest of us, you must earn your keep. It has been many years since she had a captive child in her household, but if you are a good girl and a hard worker and bring credit to the family, she will try to be patient and help you learn to talk properly. She forgives you for your rude remark." Rising Hawk smiled broadly behind the old lady's back. "I'm sorry, Livy. I should have warned you not to use it."

The old woman turned and motioned impatiently for Livy to follow. Rising Hawk stopped her. He spoke to her gently for a few moments. She seemed suspicious and then upset. Her eyes reddened with tears. She took the strap from Rising Hawk and disappeared into the longhouse.

"What did you say to her, Rising Hawk?"

"It's nothing. I explained you are a guest from my brother's house. She always cries when he is mentioned. He was her favorite grandchild, and she has not seen him in two winters. Sometimes she forgets and thinks that he is dead, but she knows there was no condolence ceremony for him. Usually when a warrior disappears like that, he's been killed, and the family asks for a captive to replace him in the family. She thought maybe you were here to dry her tears. She forgets we haven't been at war for years now. She's a little disappointed. If she tries to send you after wood again, just tell me. Don't be offended."

"Why didn't you tell me that was a bad word?"

He shrugged. "I forgot."

Livy finished eating very slowly, so slowly that Rising Hawk was nearly twitching with impatience. It was obvious he would not be able to hand her over to his grandmother. He disappeared into the longhouse again.

His grandmother was bent over the kettle, stirring.

"Our guest wore out her shoes. She needs moccasins," he said.

"She needs a bath."

"Please, Grandmother, lend her some of yours. Otherwise she will stay with you all day to help. She is very obliging and"—he touched his nose—"much worse when she warms up." Livy came in just in time to see the gesture and be puzzled by it.

The old woman reached under her sleeping compartment and

withdrew a pair of worn moccasins. As she handed them to Livy, she whispered to Rising Hawk. "Don't bother to give them back. Burn them." She snickered at her own joke.

"What did she say?" Livy asked as she bent to pull them on.

"Nothing, really," Rising Hawk said. "Except that she likes you, Livy."

Chapter 13

Rising Hawk's grandmother continued to find fault with Livy. The next morning she badgered Buffalo Creek Woman, complaining, "Take that captive girl down to the river and bathe her. It will be a kindness to the rest of us."

During four moons in his brother's household, Rising Hawk had never seen Polly or Livy swim. "Settlers' women stay out of the river," he cautioned his mother. "I believe they fear the water spirits will make them ill. They are very reluctant to wet their bodies all over."

"How do they keep clean then?" Buffalo Creek Woman asked.

Rising Hawk explained what he assumed was going on behind the curtains on those rare occasions when Polly put the washtub before the fire and shooed the men out.

His mother refused to listen to his tales of heated water and washtubs and makeshift curtains of table linen. "Foolishness," she declared. "They make work of everything." As a precaution, though, she alerted her daughters that Livy would probably run.

Late in the afternoon, Buffalo Creek Woman and her daughters escorted Livy through the village. Women were everywhere, emptying harvest baskets of dry bean pods ready for shelling, laying hold of wayward children, chatting. Polly would feel right at home here, Livy mused.

Their little procession brought only a few interested looks, some quiet greetings. News of the girl's coming had made the rounds yesterday. Some of the ladies had come by to inspect the small wheel she had carried over the mountains. A few of the sachems had informally discussed the purpose of the child's visit.

There were some unpleasant remarks directed at Buffalo Creek Woman and her upstart eldest son, but the enterprise struck them as harmless enough. The more tolerant among them even admitted it might prove useful. At any rate, it was a women's matter and none of their business.

It was a short walk downriver to the sandy swimming hole the village women had reserved for themselves. It was hot and sunny and still, for now. In the evening, the harvesters would gather to wash away the sweat and dust of a full day in the fields. At present their only company was a flock of mallard ducks near the opposite shore, paddling upstream, then lazily riding the current down.

Livy, who was prepared to pull up her sleeves and wash her face and hands, was shocked as the four women began stripping off their long, red overblouses, dark blue skirts, and moccasins. It was worse when the four descended on her and stripped her down to the skin. Rising Hawk hadn't said anything about a bath. "Go with my mother to the river. Take your other shift" were his only instructions. She'd obeyed him, thinking she would be doing her laundry.

She tried to cover herself, but Buffalo Creek Woman took her hand, crooning, "Nice. Not cold," as if she were calming an animal. Nobody pushed her in, but neither would they let her out, the two older sisters forming a barricade at her back. Livy wondered how she could explain that in civilized places there were laws against immersing fully in water. It was especially dangerous for women. These people must suffer fever and ague unending, she thought. All she could do was pray she wouldn't die.

Once in the water, Livy washed quickly, but Buffalo Creek Woman was determined to keep her submerged and soaking for as long as possible. She retrieved the girl's clothes, the ones Livy had worn for the entire journey to Jenuchshadego, and tossed them to her. Livy did the best she could without hot water and lye soap, but each time she tried to lay them on the grassy bank to dry Buffalo Creek Woman sniffed at them delicately and handed them back.

Rising Hawk lay on the downslope of the riverbank, basking in the sun. His eyes were closed as he listened to the laughter drifting up from the bathing women. When they were finished, he would take Livy around to check on their snares. She had hated the idea, but he had taken her up and down hills all yesterday, setting rabbit traps.

At his wits' end, he had conceived the idea to get her out of his grandmother's way, and out of the sight of his few friends who—because of injury, illness, or an unfavorable dream—hadn't joined the hunt. Never had he seen his grandmother take such a thorough dislike to anyone as she had to Livy. And his friends were merciless. Men and women spent very little time in each other's company. His friends were calling him "mother."

Despite her loud and frequent protests, he had been grudgingly pleased when Livy did well. Her hands were accustomed to tying knots, and once he had pointed out that she couldn't find her way back to the village without him, she was quick to learn. He had chosen a beautiful trail, and she often stood transfixed, looking out over the valley. "I feel like a bird," she said once, after a long silence. "When I was sick and dizzy, I could close my eyes and pretend I was twirling in the air. I felt it. Like I was in a high place. Same as this." She closed her eyes. She looked as if she were listening to something far away. "Did you ever wonder what it would be like to fly?"

Alarmed, Rising Hawk took her arm and made her step back, chiding her for silliness. It was curious. Livy was never fanciful. If any girl was practical, it was she. After that she said very little, but her face showed him that she was seeing with more than her eyes.

His mother and two older sisters passed him on their way back from the river. His mother praised Livy generously. "Runs Faster has her paddling in the shallows, with her head above water already."

"Barely," Takes Up the Net said, grinning. "Livy looks worried, like a squirrel that can swim when forced but would much rather climb a tree."

"At least she tries," Pretty Girl reproved her sister gently.

Buffalo Creek Woman shook a finger at Rising Hawk. "Go

away. If anyone should see you here, sneaking looks like an over-heated boy, you will have to leave the village. What a disgrace it will be for the rest of us."

"I'm waiting to take her to check some snares," Rising Hawk said sharply as the women walked away laughing.

Livy and Runs Faster were getting noisy. It sounded as if the girls were jumping from the flat boulder that rose from the shallows. Their laughter rose to shrieks suddenly, and instinctively he rolled onto his belly and looked over the edge of the riverbank.

Runs Faster was shoulder deep in the river, trying to coax Livy, who stood hesitating on the rock, into making a leap. Water streamed heavily from Livy's hair, down her back, over her legs. The sun reflected off the water. She was intensely white, like a new snowfall, and probably cold to the touch, but she was more womanly than Rising Hawk had pictured. She had grown since her illness and had rounded out nicely. He averted his eyes. It was unsettling to him, suddenly, that he had pictured her in his mind at all.

He had a friend, a woman, a Huron captive, who many years ago had married a warrior of the Wolf Clan. He had been killed in the American war. She had always been very fond of Rising Hawk, and they had been lovers some years back. Even now, he sometimes considered marrying her. His mother respected her, and it was customary for young men to marry much older women. His eyes strayed again to Livy. Perhaps this was a sign that now would be a good time to renew their friendship.

At last, Runs Faster's cajoling worked. Livy stepped off the rock almost sedately, but a last-minute tuck of the knees sent a wave over Runs Faster, who sputtered and complained loudly. Livy apologized but could not control her smile.

Rising Hawk frowned and ducked back down. It was disturbing to see her like this. Very disturbing. He knew she was a child, certainly, but how did it look to the village, his being constantly in the company of this young woman? He had taken his friends' jokes about her with good grace and a clear conscience. Suddenly he felt like a fool. His mother had put him in a very awkward position.

Below, the girls dragged themselves from the river. They stood squeezing water from their hair. Livy self-consciously struggled into her shift, getting tangled as she pulled the dry linen over her damp skin. Her other shift, overgown, apron, and stockings were spread on the grass, drying. Runs Faster made her sit as she combed her hair. She fanned it out on her shoulders to dry.

"Good," she pronounced, patting Livy's head. She leaned forward, inhaling loudly and snuffling here and there at her. "Good. Very splendid," she pronounced in her mother's fragmented English. Then she spoke in Seneca. "You smelled so badly we were afraid we would be asked to build you your own house."

Rising Hawk was waiting for them just over the bank. He looked bored and a little annoyed. Livy had behaved badly. She had been noisy and childish. It was her fault that he had looked over the riverbank at them. What if someone had seen?

"You two were squealing like pigs. And you," he said, glaring at Livy, "took too long. We were supposed to check on your snares. Now it is growing late, and we can't go or we won't get back before dark. Think of those poor, little rabbits, hanging helpless in the traps set by your own hand."

Livy flushed at the cruel taunt, but something in his expression reminded her of Gideon. He was wrong to say that and he knew it. Furious, she laid her hands on his chest and shoved. He stumbled, shocked that she had touched him like that. "*Seegwah*," she said harshly, and pushed him again. Then she brushed by with Runs Faster, and the two of them hurried off. His sister smiled sweetly as she passed.

Rising Hawk glanced around quickly to assure himself that they had not been observed. He scowled as he watched them go. If Livy was going to behave like a stubborn child, he should treat her like one. It was only because he was glad to be rid of her that he didn't pick her up, take her to the riverbank, and hold her head underwater. She had no idea how rude she had been.

Chapter 14

"If I knew just a little Seneca, I could learn the words for *jackass*, *simpleton*, *bully*, *idiot*, and *fool*. Gideon and Rising Hawk and even Polly know how to talk it. I don't know what I was thinking all these months." Runs Faster looked back at Livy, who was following her doggedly up the trail. The little one was talkative this evening. Being angry with Rising Hawk had set something free. It was very funny. Livy returned the look. "I know you can't understand me, but those are all good English words that describe your brother," she said. "Rising Hawk—is—a—f-o-o-l."

Runs Faster pointed behind Livy. Despite their protests, Rising Hawk was following them up the mountainside, from a safe distance. "Full," she said, to Livy's delight.

For the most part, the girls ignored Rising Hawk, and Livy's spirits rose as they tramped from trap to trap. They were all empty, and Rising Hawk was hungry and mad at them both for keeping him from his food. Livy was enjoying his grim expression. Then they came to the last snare.

Livy heard it before she saw it. It was a large gray and brown rabbit, twisting and jumping on the end of the rope, emitting weak screams.

Quickly she stepped on the sapling that anchored the snare, and lowered it to the ground. Her fingers shook as she untied it. "There, go on now, run," she pleaded. "Get away."

The rabbit lay still at her feet, and she realized she was too late. Runs Faster made a snapping motion with her hands. Its back was broken.

Rising Hawk looked over her shoulder. "It can't run," he said bluntly. "Kill it."

Livy shook her head. Runs Faster and Rising Hawk looked at each other in amazement. Was it possible she could be so cruel? But one look at her face told the story. She was stricken.

"You know, don't you, that an owl, or a dog, won't kill it when they find it. First, they'll eat some of it. It will die as its legs are being chewed off or its eyes pecked out."

"Don't, Rising Hawk," Livy said, dropping to her knees. Gingerly, she gathered the rabbit into her lap.

"If you kill it quickly, it will have a little fear and no more pain. Close your ears to it, then swing its head against this tree, as hard as you can."

Livy gently stroked the rabbit and shook her head. "You do it. This was your stupid idea anyway."

"Livy, you are trying my patience. I am hungry. I want to go home. Just do it."

Runs Faster stood aside, watching Livy, then her brother, as their angry words flew back and forth.

"Just take hold of its hind feet. I assure you, you are frightening it to death with your caresses anyway. It is no small thing for this rabbit to give up his life for you. Show your gratitude by giving it a quick death."

"It's a cruel way to show gratitude," Livy said, her voice strained and desperate. "This is your fault, Rising Hawk. You made me set the trap. You're the one who really caught it. You should kill it."

"Don't be a coward. The smallest child can do this. How is this possible? Before you came to Gideon, what did you eat—grass?"

The rabbit was still twitching. Livy realized it was panting. She could feel the slight pulse of its breath, quick and fluttering against her belly. Rising Hawk wasn't going to help her. He had made that clear. He had called her a coward.

Runs Faster recognized a stalemate when she saw it. Without a word she bent over Livy, caught the rabbit's furry hind legs, and swung. She rolled her eyes as she handed the rabbit to her brother, but took care that Livy shouldn't see. The sound of her brother's words had been harsh. Even without understanding their meaning, she could see Livy had been hurt by them. Despite her mother's good intentions, she would have to take the girl over. Rising Hawk was an idiot.

Over his sister's protests, Rising Hawk made Livy carry the rabbit all the way back to the village. Every time she threw it to the ground, he picked it up and forced it into her hand. Not only did a tiny stream of blood mar her dress, but the creature bumped against her legs, so she felt its soft, pliable warmth grow cold and stiff with each step.

Groups of little boys questioned Rising Hawk as they passed through the village. Each time he directed their eyes to Livy. None of them had trapped such a rabbit in these hills for many, many moons—some never. It was not pleasant to be bested by a girl. They regarded her with envy and suspicion.

In the longhouse his grandmother turned a quizzical eye on Livy.

"You caught this rabbit?" Rising Hawk translated.

Livy nodded glumly. "Rising Hawk forced me to. He ought to be ashamed of himself. He's been nasty and cruel all day."

Rising Hawk was silent.

"Well, well," the old lady said, her voice tinged with sarcasm. "She makes cloth from grass and hunts like a boy. She is a very clever girl." She turned to her daughter. "Take her into the fields tomorrow," she said in an undertone to Buffalo Creek Woman. "Your son has no sense of propriety. What will he do next? Pluck her head, give her a tomahawk, and take her raiding? This is scandalous. Everyone will say she is unnatural." She peered grimly at Livy as she steered her out the longhouse door to the butchering place.

Rising Hawk smiled smugly as he stretched out in his sleeping compartment. He had rid himself of the child without having to take the blame. He had done it without breaking his promise to Polly, and he hadn't even planned it. An eventful day. He fell asleep...free.

The women harvested together, under the direction of a matron elected to be overseer. They would pick the first row in one field, then move on to do the first row in the next field, and so on. When the first row of every field and plot belonging to the village had been done, they went back and picked all the second rows, until each farm had been harvested fairly.

Livy was grateful to be allowed to join the happy, laughing crowd and to hear the songs and chatter, even if she understood little of it. Rising Hawk had been a resentful guardian, but the women welcomed her heartily. And when Runs Faster managed to teach her the simple refrain to one of their songs, they all agreed she was a good sport.

Some of the women, the older ones in particular, worked shirtless in the old Seneca fashion. Livy was scandalized at her first glimpse of a grandmother half-naked. As she harvested alongside Runs Faster, she tried to imagine the farm women in Conway, Massachusetts, imitating the Seneca matrons in their dress.

"You can't understand me, can you?" she asked. "You know a few words, like your mother, but not enough to matter."

Runs Faster looked over and smiled. She thought Livy knew she couldn't understand her. What was she saying now? She hoped this wouldn't necessitate putting down her basket and going in search of her brother.

"It's just that I'm not used to seeing people naked, except for babies. I can't imagine my Aunt Mary working in her flower garden without her bodice. Or the ladies going to church in gloves and bonnets, but no tops. That would finish the congregation. Or Mrs. Wilkes. She's a little stout. Actually she's very stout. What if Mrs. Wilkes did her housework half-naked?" At the thought of that grim, prim matron bustling about with her bosom unbound, Livy broke into helpless giggles and sat, nearly choking, at the base of a cornstalk to laugh it out.

The hunters had returned, and Rising Hawk was relieved to be able to settle into his usual pastimes. Livy caught sight of him in a group of young men going down to the river. Later she saw him target shooting on the edge of the field the women were harvesting. When he reappeared that evening, he ignored her until his mother gave him a sign that he was needed to translate, and even then he escaped as soon as possible. Livy felt slighted. Rising Hawk seemed unapproachable now, as if they were on opposite sides of a stockade fence. After the rabbit episode, she felt she was the one with a grievance, but he acted as if she had offended him.

That evening there was a gathering to prepare food for the Green Corn Festival. Runs Faster handed Livy a scraper made of a deer jaw, and the two of them set to scraping the milky corn kernels off the cobs. It reminded Livy of harvest at home in Conway, when everyone would help put up the crops and share music and stories. Tonight many of the men showed up, and none seemed reluctant to help. Livy observed that during the socializing and singing, the normally reserved Seneca were very flirtatious.

Rising Hawk sat with an older woman Livy took to be an aunt. But she also noticed a certain young woman, very pretty, who kept her eye on Rising Hawk and contrived, at one point, to reach for an ear of corn at exactly the same time he did, brushing his hand and saying something that made him smile shyly.

Runs Faster saw it, too, and nudged Livy.

"Sassafras," she whispered, and fluttered her eyes in her brother's direction. Runs Faster laid a hand over her heart, and the girls laughed. Rising Hawk looked up at their giggling just in time to see Livy smirking at him. He came to them quickly and snatched the scraper from Livy's hand as he knelt next to her.

"You have been working all day," he said, glaring at her. His voice was loud and scolding. "I think you should go home and go to sleep. You are so tired you are behaving like a child—a bad child." He paused for effect. "You should go before everyone notices." He threw the scraper down and stalked off. Runs Faster pretended to be deeply absorbed in her work.

Livy picked up her scraper, blinking back tears. It felt as if the eyes of the entire village were on her. She continued her work, feeling the shame of public humiliation creep over her face.

Timidly, she looked up. No one seemed to be paying any attention, but she knew that the chattering and laughter was quieter. She laid down her work and left the group.

Livy ran down the dark path. The night was cool, and if she hadn't been afraid of what lay outside the village, she would have kept running. The longhouse was empty, the fires banked and low. She climbed into her sleeping compartment and, grateful for a rare moment of solitude, gave way to her loneliness.

Of course, none of this was lost on the rest of the village. While Livy drifted through the days, isolated by language, and thinking herself invisible, she was being keenly observed.

They approved of her reserve and thought her polite, but felt she lacked an independent spirit. They also felt that perhaps Rising Hawk's mother was throwing the two young people together too much. It was unnatural for a man and a woman to be in each other's company that often. Witness this spat tonight. Now the Yankee girl would want to leave the village before she showed them how to take the tall grass the settlers grew and turn it into cloth. Perhaps Buffalo Creek Woman was meddling too much. No one had asked her to arrange this.

Buffalo Creek Woman witnessed the disagreement and saw Livy leave. It disturbed her to see Rising Hawk overreact to the girl's teasing. He rarely acknowledged such conduct from his sisters. Was it possible? No, it seemed beyond possibility that Rising Hawk felt an attraction to the little girl. Likely he didn't care to be embarrassed while sitting between Sassafras and Twisted Hair, the Huron widow.

But it wouldn't hurt to have a talk with Sassafras's grandmother. It was a little unusual for a man and a woman so close in age to marry. Sassafras was twenty-five, and Rising Hawk nearly twenty. But times were changing and Sassafras came from an important family. Her sons could be chosen to be sachems. Rising Hawk's ability to translate at council fires had earned him favor. There were many in the village who had their eye upon him. Women from very important families, some of them. If Sassafras's grandmother wished to follow tribal tradition and pair the girl with an older, steadier man, say a widower of fifty or sixty, those other women could be approached.

Perhaps it was her fault, for insisting he look after Livy. Some of the gossips were suggesting that her youngest was going to follow his brother's example and become a white man. That riled her, but the best way to deal with nonsense of that sort was to ignore it. Meanwhile, she would talk to a few grandmothers, do a little arranging. It would be a nice surprise for Rising Hawk, and a relief to her.

Chapter 15

John Gage rambled in four days after the Seneca relations left. His clothes were in a shambles and he was hungover, but as disordered as his life was, he never missed a corn harvest. He loathed the work, but loved Gideon. It was the only obligation that could ever tear him away from what he considered his true calling: perfecting his method for aging dangerously potent applejack. It was renowned in three counties for having brought a cholera victim back to life.

With luck, they would be a sufficient harvest crew, as long as Gideon could keep Ephraim contained until it was over. The visit from the family had all but ruined him for farmwork.

Polly was fit to be tied. She'd tried to fill in for Livy's absence with Ephraim, but on the second day he had let the fire burn out. The fourth day the cows went unmilked. Now this morning, only five days since Livy had gone and taken Polly's peace of mind with her, Ephraim had wandered off and left the samp to scorch. One look at the blackened mess in the bottom of the kettle, and she'd sat down and cried. Gideon found her when he came in from milking.

"All I wanted was a decent breakfast. We can't harvest all morning on a cup of tea," she said, tears streaming down her face. "I only needed a few more minutes to sleep. He got Henry up and left him to mind the fire."

"Where is he now?"

"Henry said he went to check his fish trap. I'm sorry. I'm just not feeling well this morning." She avoided Gideon's eyes.

"I know," he said quietly. So far it was unspoken between them, but he feared she was pregnant again.

"Go on back to bed, honey. I'll bring you some tea in a little while and fix the children their breakfast. Get some sleep now. It's nothing that sleep can't cure. Don't fret."

"I'm sorry," she whispered, taking his hand. She rose with as much dignity as she could muster and crept off to bed.

Gideon tracked Ephraim a few hundred yards upstream. He was just dropping a stringer of trout into the creek. When Eph saw Gideon's face, he didn't dare move.

"You left a four-year-old in charge of a cooking fire? Don't you have any sense?" Gideon's voice was tight, his words clipped as he pulled Eph to his feet. "I have to be able to rely on you! Don't you understand that? No one's very tough on you here. You should be grateful. I could make it a lot harder."

Ephraim backed up a little and mumbled, "I'm sorry."

"I'm sick of your kind of 'sorry.' It never means anything."

Gideon kept hold of him all the way back to the barn, stopping only to break off a maple switch about the width of his thumb.

Inside the barn, Gideon stood in shadow, stripping the twigs from the switch. "Let's just get this over with. Take it off." His voice was harsh.

"My shirt?" No one had ever whipped him before. Eph's mouth went dry and his hands shook, but he wisely stifled his impulse to bargain, and pulled his shirt over his head.

"I'm going to tell you once, and that's the last warning you'll get from me. If you disobey anyone on this farm again, or dare to put my children in danger, you're going back to Wilkes . . . alone. Turn around."

It was cold in the shadows. Ephraim felt goose bumps rise on his arms. He stuck his fists in his armpits and took a shuddering breath.

The first blow nearly knocked him off his feet. His hands went forward, catching the wall. He didn't have time to even feel that first stroke before there was another, just as hard.

Panicked, he spun around. The switch nearly caught him on

the chin. Gideon cursed. He grabbed Eph by the neck and pinned him under his arm. The switch rose and fell eight more times.

"Damn your stubbornness, Eph," Gideon said finally, releasing him and letting the stick clatter to the floor. The welts on the boy's back unsettled him. He'd never struck a child before. His own father, his uncle would never beat a child. A Seneca boy might kill himself over treatment like this.

Eph was shaking and breathing hard. Gideon put a hand on his shoulder to steady him. "Get dressed. Then get yourself settled down. We've got work."

It pained him to see the boy nod fearfully at him. It was a whipped-dog look that shamed them both.

Some time passed before Eph would move. It hurt to raise his arms for his sleeves, and it hurt even more once his shirt was on, but he guessed it would be worse for Polly and John to see the welts. He'd rather put up with a little sting and burn than have anyone see. The thought of little Henry, who looked up to him, knowing he'd gotten a whipping made him sick.

He crept out into the yard and was relieved that no one was about. He knelt down at the creek for a drink, and splashed water over his face. He'd been determined not to cry, but it had hurt. He'd made plenty of noise.

No sounds came from the cabin. He guessed the whole family had gone to the fields. He listened for a while. He knew they needed him. They had ten acres to harvest, but he was too ashamed. The thought of facing them so soon was more than he could stand. Tears of self-pity gathered in his eyes.

He wondered if maybe Livy wouldn't be glad to see him. She hadn't been very eager to go and might find his presence comforting. Gideon had said it was a hundred miles, but Eph didn't believe it. Gideon had just told him that to make him stay put. Gideon knew how jealous he'd been of Livy's good fortune. Actually living in an Indian town! He knew he could track them down. Rising Hawk had taught him well. He had spent hours crawling along the ground scouting out the trails Rising Hawk laid for him. Even after five days, it would be easy picking up the trail of a dozen people who weren't trying to hide their tracks. He cheered up at the thought of how pleased Rising Hawk would be that his training had paid off.

It didn't take long for him to rifle the pantry. One of Polly's kitchen knives would be good enough for now. He was careful not to take her favorite. His eyes settled on John's tinderbox up on the mantle, and he hesitated only a moment before reaching up and taking it. Then he went into the bedroom and stood on the bed to reach into the rafters, where Gideon had put his bow.

He pulled a blanket from John's bed before the fireplace and rolled the things up in it. Then he looked around for a nice length of rope. There was a coil in the barn, but he was reluctant to go into the yard, unless he was running full speed for cover. Someone might come back looking for him. He was stumped until he remembered his rabbit traps in the woods. There was plenty of rope if he knotted the pieces together. He could take the traps apart on his way out.

He was relieved to find the yard still empty. He had half expected little Henry to come looking for him. He sprinted down the path, across a harvested cornfield, and into the woods.

When he was hidden by the trees, he turned and looked back on the homestead. He thought of the others, harvesting all day with the sun beating down on them. He wondered at his conscience. All he felt was pure and simple pleasure at leaving it all behind. Anyway, it wouldn't be for long. He'd come back with Livy. Meanwhile, it would serve Gideon right for hitting him so hard. He turned his back and set his feet on the trail. Maybe after he was gone a few weeks, they'd be grateful to have him back.

Chapter 16

The traps were all empty. There had been a lot of activity in the forest lately. The road crew had started felling trees in June, laying them down as they went. Jockey Road, they called it. The logs made for a bumpy ride. It was a large crew, and they made rapid progress. The rabbits had gotten cautious.

Ephraim was pleased. He needed the rope and didn't want to be slowed down any. He was only an hour's tramp from the homestead, and there was always the chance that someone would discover he had gone and come after him.

He was so absorbed in untying a trap that he didn't even notice the three workmen coming up the trail until they called out to him. "Where'd you come from, boy?" a dusty man in a tricorn hat asked. "You ain't on the crew."

Ephraim took in the three men, the axes, and the dust and concluded they were just looking for a place to relieve themselves after dinner. No cause for alarm. "Yonder," he said vaguely. "You working on the new road?"

"Yup," answered a gentleman in a coonskin cap, who stepped up to a white pine and turned his back.

"I didn't know there was a place over this way," said the third. He had a three-days' growth of beard and was still holding a hunk of journey cake in his fist. "Course, I don't know this section too well. Might settle down here, though, if I can coax a few acres off the local squires got this place sewed up. They sell the tracts awful big around here."

The tricorn looked over Ephraim's shoulder at the trap. "That's different. Where'd you learn to set a trap like that?"

The gentleman with the journey cake spat into the dust, close to Ephraim's knee, and grunted.

"My master's folks came by for a visit awhile ago," Ephraim said, pulling out a knot with a flourish a magician might envy. "They practically ate us out of house and home, so I set extra traps. We needed the game. His father showed me this new one. It's kind of tricky."

The two men exchanged amused looks.

"Your master's father must be Seneca then," declared the gentleman in coonskin, turning around. "That there's a Seneca trap."

"Yes, sir, he is. He showed me lots of Indian things."

"I'll wager he did, young fella."

Eph felt rather than heard a subtle change in the man's voice. Suddenly he was too clumsy to tie the rope lengths together. His hands were trembling.

The gentleman in the tricorn opened his mouth to say something, but the coonskin motioned him to be quiet.

"How many of these Seneca came visiting?" He spoke to Ephraim's back as the boy knelt, quickly winding up rope and making a mess of it.

"Only a few," Eph said cautiously. "They were hardly here at all. Just a night or two." He bound the coil with a final twist.

The coonskin stepped in front of Eph, coming between him and his bundle. "Only a few, and they cleaned out your supplies? And this fella had time to teach you traps? Nice of him. Any other warriors?"

"Just him," Eph lied, "and he was about a hundred years old. He's probably not much of one anymore. He talked, mostly."

"That so? What did he talk about?"

"I don't know," Eph said, frustration seeping into his voice. "I don't speak Seneca."

"Folks in town know about these Seneca coming and going at your place?"

"I don't know. What's the difference?"

The man finishing up his dinner snorted. "Well, there's a little matter of them marauding Shawnee from the west. There's rumors that Seneca been going along with them."

Ephraim stood up and hung the coiled rope from his shoulder. It burned like a slow fire. "I didn't see any Shawnee." His voice faltered as he stepped around the coonskin and bent quickly to pick up his bundle. "They're way off in Kentucky or Ohio or Pennsylvania, hundreds of miles from here." The men were silent. "I didn't see any Shawnee." Before he could take another step, the coonskin grabbed him.

"And wouldn't know them if you did. You don't know your backside from a hole in the ground. I ain't willing to let a pup like you tell me what's what. I reckon there are some folks in town you ought to talk to."

"No, sir, I . . . I don't think so," Eph stammered. "If you'd please let go. I'd best be home real soon, or my master'll skin me alive."

"No, he won't. He'll need to be worrying about his own skin, if any of this tale you've told us turns out to be true. We only just got shed of them Seneca, and we mean to stay shed."

Ephraim tried to pull free. The coonskin held tight and smiled slightly. Ephraim pulled a little harder and at the same time aimed a kick at the man's privates. Eph's bundle went flying as the coonskin doubled over and Ephraim ducked to avoid an arm stretched out to grab him. He spun around sharp and went face first into the belly of the man with the beard. They both went down. Ephraim landed with a grunt on the man's abdomen. Next thing he knew, someone was hauling him up by the neck, a fist was drawn back in front of his face, and the two other men were roaring with laughter.

The fist hung in the air just inches from his nose. It had long, curling fingernails, permanently blackened with dirt. Eph knew about that. Some frontiersmen grew their nails long on purpose, for gouging a man's eye out in a fight. The man saw him looking. He opened his fist and brought two fingers up to Eph's left eye. Eph winced as the nails dug slightly into his cheek.

"You should hear 'em scream, boy. Even makes me sick, sometimes, to hear it. It just goes on and on." He smiled, and Ephraim felt his knees start to give.

"Now hold on, Lawson. No need to maul the infant. You startled him. It was just natural he should fight back."

Slowly Lawson loosened his grip.

"You ever get a notion to try that again, boy, I'll take that eye out and make you eat it." He gave Eph a shove.

Ephraim stumbled back into the tricorn, who steadied him, picked up Eph's scattered belongings, and headed back toward the road. Lawson pointed with a blackened nail. There was nothing Ephraim could do but follow.

Chapter 17

The first day of Green Corn Festival, Rising Hawk left early, before eating, in the company of some other young men. He said nothing to Livy, but looked cautiously her way a few times. Runs Faster recognized it as one of her brother's subtler forms of apology. Livy ignored him.

Right after the family's morning meal, Buffalo Creek Woman took Livy aside and tried to cheer her with a description of what they would see that day. Without Rising Hawk, it had to be done in pantomime. Livy came away with the impression that they would spend the day dancing while people circled them and either played some kind of instrument, or ate dinner. She couldn't be sure which.

It looked as if the entire village had gathered at the council house. Buffalo Creek Woman and the girls mingled with the crowd, discussing this and that, while Livy tagged along.

She circled the wooden statue of the Creator, Tarachiawagon, that dominated the yard before the council house door. It was decorated with ribbons and feathers and odd bits of things she couldn't identify. She wondered what her uncle would have to say about her going to worship with a bunch of idolaters. She was afraid to so much as touch it, as if something dark and dangerous might rub off onto her.

She recognized Sassafras from the evening before and noticed that Rising Hawk's mother bestowed a great deal of attention on the girl and had a lengthy conversation with a woman Livy presumed was the girl's mother. Although she hadn't noticed before, she decided Sassafras had an unpleasant, sly look about her, and her teeth were too prominent. They stuck out, in fact. That discovery made Livy smile, and she was ashamed of herself the next moment, as Sassafras returned her smile graciously.

The milling crowd eventually made its way into the council house, the men occupying benches on one side of the house and the women occupying the other. Livy had barely been seated next to Runs Faster when a group of women took the center floor for a ceremony that involved babies being brought forward by their parents. The women spoke at length over each child; it seemed to Livy to be some kind of christening ceremony.

After the babies, two men with turtle-shell rattles took up places at either end of a bench in the middle of the floor and began to pound out a beat. Almost immediately a long file of male dancers entered through the doorway at the men's end. They were attired in their best kilts, leggings, and moccasins. Each garment was embellished by embroidery. Across each bare chest, descending from the left shoulder, was a long woven sash. Decorated bands of animal skin were tied to their upper arms, wrists, and knees. Several of the dancers wore knee rattles of deer hooves or silver bells. A few of the men wore headdresses of leather caps adorned with eagle and pheasant feathers.

Livy's heart beat almost as fast as the rattles as she watched the dancers winding their way up one side of the house and then down the other. Although none of the movements were threatening, the strange clothes brought to mind all her uncle's fearsome stories.

Runs Faster was amused. Livy was nearly a woman and frightened by noise. She was lucky this was not a False Face ceremony or, worse yet, a war dance. Even Runs Faster found a war dance frightening.

At that precise moment the drummers increased the beat. The dancers increased their stomping, and the crowd began to sway along with them. Runs Faster felt Livy swaying next to her.

An old man had taken the floor and advanced to a fire pit. Scattering some tobacco leaves on the flames, he held up his hands. As the rattles abruptly ceased, he addressed the crowd in a clear, resonant voice. The people settled in, and Livy felt as though she were in a meetinghouse in Conway.

Across the council house, seated nearly opposite the women of the family, Livy caught sight of Rising Hawk. His face was so stern he might have been a deacon back home, scanning the congregation for signs of impiety, but Livy could see he was returning her impudent stare. She tried to outstare him, but he seemed to know what she was about and wouldn't blink. She let her hands stray to her face. Without smiling, she pulled down on her lower eyelids and stuck out her tongue. She stayed that way for a long time, causing the young men on either side of Rising Hawk to frown and jostle him with their elbows. She didn't stop until Runs Faster noticed her disrespectful behavior and slapped her hands down.

There was a ball game that afternoon. Livy and Runs Faster roamed the crowds together, with Runs Faster stopping to chat with women and girls and introducing Livy as they went. It was Runs Faster who elbowed her way through the crowd to find them a spot in front. She smiled proudly and pointed to a player at the far end of the field, holding his stick high in the air and running like mad in their direction. "Rising Hawk," she said, nudging Livy's shoulder and pointing again.

It was Rising Hawk, with at least a dozen players in his wake. He covered half the length of the field, while the crowd hooted and hollered, tossing hats and tomahawks into the air. There was a mad crush right in front of Livy where several players contested for the ball. In the midst of the confusion, she saw Rising Hawk recover the ball and step back. Before he could make his escape, several players tumbled into him, and they all went down in a heap, Rising Hawk at the bottom.

Runs Faster screamed with laughter as her brother disentangled himself from the pile. Livy was impassive, ignoring the melee in front of her, scanning the horizon as if she were interested in the weather. One of the players had a gash on his head, and blood poured from it. He stumbled off the field as another player ran in to take his place. Livy turned and strolled off while the substitution was being made.

Rising Hawk got to his feet soon after. Runs Faster saw him watch Livy's retreat. He looked puzzled, then, surprisingly, disappointed. No one but Runs Faster was able to read his face so well, and she found it hard to believe. As improbable as it seemed, Rising Hawk was noticing Livy. Runs Faster smiled to herself. Her grandmother would make a terrific fuss and take to her bed. If their mother had plans, she had better execute them at once. Rising Hawk had stopped the play in front of Livy on purpose. She wondered how Sassafras would react to that. The gossips would see to it that the news got back to her by nightfall.

The food they had prepared communally the night before was fetched home at twilight by the women as each family feasted at its own fireside. Along with the corn, beans, and squash, the succotash that evening contained bear meat. Livy found herself overeating when she discovered the mixture of sweet green corn with berries and chopped apples that came wrapped in corn husks. After eating, the entire village returned to the council house. Runs Faster, remembering Livy's excitement at seeing the feather dance, dragged her into the first group of dancers that she could.

Livy was reluctant, staggering and slightly behind the beat. She trailed Runs Faster like a drunken shadow, begging to be let off. But Runs Faster was determined. She endured several heel-bruising collisions, until Livy learned to hop on the twelfth beat instead of shuffle forward.

The drum rhythm kept time with the heartbeat of each woman in the stomping, shuffling circle, but Livy was oblivious to their communion. The Peltons were Congregationalists. Dancing, cards, and hard liquor were sins. Now here she was, dancing with heathens. The worst of it was, God knew her heart. And right now she was enjoying herself.

Sassafras was at the dance that evening. She made a point of greeting Livy and being pleasant. She even placed herself next to Livy for the women's dance and helped her keep in line. Sheepishly, Livy had to admit that Sassafras was neither ugly nor sly. Actually, done up as she was in her best clothes and jewelry, she was the prettiest woman there.

It was during the women's dance that Rising Hawk came into view among a group of young men. They were looking over the girls and trying to appear as if they were not. Sassafras shone like a full moon in all her finery. Dancing beside her, Livy felt self-conscious in her everyday dress. She wished, suddenly, that she were pretty, and that Rising Hawk would notice, that they all would notice and admire her. When the drums stopped, Livy slipped away.

It was well past midnight when Livy waved good-night to Runs Faster. She stepped outside and took a deep breath to clear away the gloom. Melancholy clung to her like the smoky smell that permeated the village. She wished Rising Hawk's mother would hold the spinning demonstration and get it over with. She yearned to go home. She wanted to talk to Polly. She couldn't talk about it here. Especially to Rising Hawk.

The smells of cooking and of sweating bodies were strong even in the night air. People were coming and going as if it were a market night in Conway. One friendly circle was passing the whiskey jug and motioned for her to join them. She shook her head in what she hoped was a polite refusal and trudged away. Then, as if her melancholy was not deep enough, Rising Hawk appeared suddenly, falling into step with her as soon as she was far enough away from the council house door to be in shadow. It was a bitter revelation. Not only was he not fond of her, he was even ashamed to be seen with her.

They walked a fair distance in silence before Rising Hawk finally said, "Last night I was rude to you. My sister said you were angry."

Her face grew hot as it always did at the realization that people had been discussing her. "I didn't really notice."

Rising Hawk knew this was an outright lie. She had been furious. She had scowled at him all morning and made herself look ridiculous this afternoon in the council house, just to embarrass him. He had had real difficulty in suppressing his laughter. His Huron widow and Sassafras were lovely women, but predictable. Neither of them would have risked looking as foolish as she had in public. He had never thought of Livy as reckless before tonight.

"You know," he said cheerily, changing the subject, "you danced the women's dance a little well."

"Which one was that?"

"The one with Sassafras. You face this way." He demonstrated.

"No, I didn't. I ran into her and stomped on her heel."

"Don't be obstinate. You did well. It is new to you, after all. We start dancing as soon as we can walk—before really, on our mothers' backs. You were fine for someone with no experience. You were not nearly as clumsy as I expected you to be."

"Thank you. That's a charming compliment."

Rising Hawk smiled, pleased to think he had done something right. "Sassafras seems very fond of you. She looked nice tonight, don't you think?"

"Nice? She was the prettiest girl there, Rising Hawk."

"Many of the men admire her."

"Of course."

"Her mother hasn't picked a husband for her yet. Many are hopeful. Her family, her grandmother, is very important."

"Can't she pick her own husband?"

Rising Hawk smiled indulgently. "Of course not. The mothers and grandmothers decide. Very often, it is a pleasant surprise. My parents did not even know each other until the bride bread was delivered."

"You mean to tell me, your mama will pick your wife?"

"Usually your grandmother decides. The clan matrons have a great deal of influence as well."

Livy was silent, wondering just how seriously the family would take Rising Hawk's grandmother's advice when the time came. She hoped they would have the sense to disregard it.

"What happens if you prefer another lady and they won't allow you to marry her?"

"That rarely happens. Besides, why would you want someone your whole family thinks would be bad for you?"

"If that's so, then why do you suppose the girls get all decked out for the dances?"

"Decked out?"

"All dressed up with their geegaws and such. And if nobody gets to pick, why does Sassafras sashay around you like this?" Livy cut across the path in a fair imitation of the older girl's walk.

"That is simply the way she walks. Grown women walk like that."

"Your mother doesn't," Livy said casually. "Hardly anyone does, Rising Hawk. You can't keep water in a bucket, bumping around like that."

Rising Hawk made no reply. Clearly she was laughing at him. He would have considered it rude in anyone else. It was odd how Livy's bad behavior sometimes struck him as charming. Livy had been in his thoughts for much of the day and night. This had led him to take a drink of whiskey during the women's dance. The drink had made him reckless. If she had not disappeared right afterward, he might have gone to her side for the dance with joined hands. It was the only time unmarried men and women touched publicly. It would not have passed unnoticed. Nothing ever did. But right now, under cover of darkness and slightly drunk, he didn't care.

Chapter 18

Livy was the only sleeper in the longhouse to be awakened next morning by the argument. The other revelers had come in at dawn and were dead to the world.

The sound of Rising Hawk's voice, low but forceful, nudged her out of a dream and into a sitting position. Just beyond the deerskin curtain that made the sleeping platform a private compartment, Buffalo Creek Woman's voice rose in anger. Rising Hawk answered her sharply. Livy's stomach tensed. Snuggling into her blankets, she tried to ignore them, but the voices were too close. Hardly thinking, she scrambled into her clothes and out of the compartment.

They were standing by the fire pit and looked up indignantly as she passed, but she kept her head down and said nothing. They resumed their argument as soon as she was through the doorway.

The river was deserted as Livy made her way down the sandy banks. In the shallows there was a flat-topped boulder that barely cleared the river's surface. Lifting her skirts to her waist, she waded into the water and climbed up to watch the sunrise.

The first she knew of Rising Hawk's presence was a splash upstream, behind her. She startled, and a short squeak escaped her as he sat down next to her.

"What's wrong with you?" he jeered. "Are your ears full of clay?"

Livy didn't respond. Sitting as close as they were, she could hear him grinding his teeth. "Women think of nothing but marriage," he said.

"Not me."

Rising Hawk snorted. "You are not a woman, Livy. You are nearly an infant."

"I'm just turned fifteen, Rising Hawk. Old enough to think about it, if I was inclined."

"Well, most women think of nothing else."

"You don't know anything about girls, Rising Hawk. Your grandmother's in charge of that. It's just your vanity makes you think women are all on fire to get a man in their beds."

Rising Hawk blushed a little. Livy was being a little too outspoken about things that shouldn't be mentioned. At least, not between them. "As I said, you are a baby."

"My aunt used to say that the men have all the fun and the women have all the babies." This time she was the one to blush.

Rising Hawk laughed. "She must have had reason to worry about you to say such a thing." He looked her up and down, as if he were appraising a cow. He shook his head. "I don't know why, but she was trying to scare you. To keep you from disgracing your family. Believe me, women have fun, too. You're just too young to know what I'm talking about."

"You're disgusting."

"It was you who started it," he said dryly. "Your own mother probably had fun, Livy, or you wouldn't be here. Don't look shocked; wouldn't it please you to think so?"

"It killed her, Rising Hawk!"

"Yes. That was very sad. I'm sorry; but really, Livy. Girls who are grown-up, who understand life, like men."

"Well, maybe somewhere there are a few men worth liking, but I doubt it."

Rising Hawk absorbed the insult and smiled at her tolerantly, as if she were simpleminded. It was a tactic that never failed to make her mad.

"I'm never going to marry. I'll have my own place and look

after it, and there won't be some *half-witted* man telling me what to do every blessed minute of my life."

Rising Hawk appeared to seriously consider her idea. "There will be difficulties. For example, when they hear you won't kill them, you'll be overrun with rabbits. They will eat your garden. And then there is the problem of how you will clear all those trees and build your own house. And, of course, you will have to hunt for yourself and kill more than rabbits. You are being silly, you know, Livy."

"You're the one being silly. Spinsters can hire out to spin and weave and make money. There are ways to run a farm without having a man in your bed."

"You like to talk about beds," Rising Hawk said, smiling slightly, "yet you are afraid of having babies. Well, do not be concerned. That is not unusual in a young girl. Courage grows with experience. There is plenty of time." He gave her a sidelong glance before saying, "I can assure you, it will be many years before any man looks at you with that thought in mind."

Suddenly her face was grave.

"I didn't mean that, Livy. I'm just having fun. You are not that unpleasant to look at. You are actually nice-looking in the firelight, or now, with the sun rising."

"I like sunrise," she said quietly, "and I plan on seeing eighty years of them. My mother saw twenty-five years of sunrises and died birthing me. That's not enough. Five of my aunt's friends died in childbed. Not one of them over thirty."

Rising Hawk was shocked into silence. If he was understanding her, it was a momentous decision to be made so young. Yet it was very like her. He could picture her sitting in the firelight with her needle, a solitary figure in Gideon's household, tying off her thread, making a vow.

"Have you had a dream about this?" he said finally.

"No."

"Then how can you know you will die? What signs have you seen? Who told you this?"

"No one had to tell me, Rising Hawk. It's just common sense."

"But someone bore your mother, didn't she? You had to have a grandmother."

"Perhaps it killed her, too. She died long before I was born."

"You said that the warrior who tortured himself because of a dream was wrong. That even if he hadn't done what the dream asked, he would have lived a long life anyway. Isn't this the same thing? What if you give up having a baby, and it happens that it was safe for you, that you were meant to be the mother of many children?"

"Then I guess I'll never know."

"But children are the greatest joy of life."

"Maybe there are other joys."

"If all women felt like you, there would be no more life."

"Then I guess it's lucky I'm a little unusual. Look away a moment." Livy gathered her skirts up high and slipped into the water. She paused, watching a blue heron taking slow, regal steps as it hunted across the river.

"And what happens if someday you meet a man who fills your mind and heart so that you can't think clearly? What will you do if for some unaccountable reason, this unfortunate man feels the same about you?"

"There are ways of loving your friends and showing it without being carnal. Jesus did it." She dropped her skirts as she reached the sandy bank. Rising Hawk eased off the rock and followed her.

"But you are nothing like a holy man, you know. You have unkind thoughts. They show clearly in your face. You think no one can see, but I can. Wait." Rising Hawk climbed the bank to where Livy stood, her wet feet coated with sand. Sand fleas bit her ankles. He reached into his shirt and brought out a silver brooch. It was tied to a leather string to make a necklace.

"Last night, at the dance, the other girls had ornaments. 'Gee-gaws,' you called them." He smiled and held the necklace out to her.

"It's for me?"

"Yes. Your clothes are too plain. Next time, you will have a gee-gaw to shine in, like the others."

She pulled the string over her head. "It's nice."

"We're friends now, aren't we, Livy? I don't mean because of that." Rising Hawk pointed at the brooch. "I mean because we understand each other."

"I'd be pleased to think so," Livy said quietly.

"I will hunt for you, from time to time, when you are a white-haired crazy woman living in the forest, frightening children."

"I'm not crazy, Rising Hawk."

"No, not completely. But you will be."

Livy laughed and ran up the path to escape the fleas.

Rising Hawk followed at a sedate pace. "I want to tell you, my mother is suddenly eager to marry me off. She thinks Sassafras would make an excellent wife."

"She probably will."

"Yes. She's a pleasant person, but I am a little like you. Marriage doesn't interest me. Not yet. My father was twenty-five winters when he married his first wife. My uncle, twenty-nine. It would be unusual for me to marry so young."

"Is everyone mad at you now?"

"I don't think so. Anyway, no one has baked bride bread yet."

"And if they do?"

Rising Hawk searched her face before shrugging. "I'll have to make sure no one eats it."

Chapter 19

Rising Hawk listened to his uncle, Stands Ready, with a bowed head. Rising Hawk's father had not been consulted regarding his son's odd behavior. Marriages were easily dissolved, and children belonged to their mother's clan. Maternal uncles were a constant in a boy's life, responsible for both his education and discipline. Stands Ready had rarely had problems with Rising Hawk, but the boy's mother and grandmother were keeping the household in an uproar over his refusal to marry Sassafras.

"Those meddlesome women will give me no peace until I talk to you, nephew, and now we are late for the peach-stone game. Everyone is there except us. This is all due to your obstinacy. What is the matter with you?"

"I'm sorry they've troubled you, Uncle, but they are at fault, not me. Why should they want to marry me off so soon? No other man my age is even thinking of being married. It's they who are obstinate. They should never have spoken to her grandmother."

"Sassafras is a good girl, hardworking, good-natured, and very beautiful of body. Everyone wants her. How is it you find her displeasing?"

"She is not displeasing, Uncle. I just do not wish to be married yet."

Stands Ready sighed and shook his head. "That is not what the village is saying."

"Really? What are they saying?"

"They are saying that you meet this girl from your brother's household in secret." Stands Ready paused to fill his pipe and observe his nephew's reaction.

Rising Hawk hooted. "Livy?" He looked at his uncle again, just to be sure he was serious. "We don't meet in secret. How could anyone think we . . . ? After all, Uncle, I have had lovers before. Women who are beautiful and pleasant and want me. I can assure you, she is not one of them."

"You are teaching her to hunt. Is it not an unnatural thing for a woman to learn to hunt? I find her behavior a little peculiar. She should spend more time with your mother."

"She spends time with the women, but she can't talk to them like she can to me."

His uncle blew out a thin ribbon of smoke. "I agree with Red Jacket regarding whites. It is best to stay away from them, and their religion."

"I am well aware of your views, Uncle. I agree with them. But Livy is just one harmless girl. Besides, aren't most of the Mohawk at least part white? We don't shun them."

"Yes. But we should. Look at the trouble they brought us, supporting the British. We would still have a united confederacy but for those Mohawks."

Rising Hawk was silent. He hated to set his uncle off on one of his tirades.

"And would you be a Mohawk, Nephew? When we were strong, and held the trade routes and could make whole nations ours, then the whites were useful. They could be controlled, and we were more powerful through our trade with them. Things are different now. There will soon be more whites than Haudenosaunee, Miami, Cherokee, or Shawnee all together. Their women are as prolific as robins. How do their men have any energy left for war? It is most unseemly. Would it please you to leave and adopt their ways?"

"No, of course not, Uncle. But you seem to forget that our great-grandfather was French. Besides, Gideon follows many of the whites' customs and still lives as he pleases."

"Gideon. Well, it is a disappointment to me and your father, but outwardly he is white. If he chooses to pretend to be one of them, he can make that choice. You cannot. But he is not always happy with what he has chosen. And he *cannot* live as he pleases. You know the extent of his fields. He must work all the time to keep them in order. Do you think he can hunt or fish whenever he wishes to? He keeps animals he must tend every day. And his neighbors do not accept him as one of them. They do not give him the assistance he needs. He must pay for assistance. I find that very strange. If the whites are so stingy with one of their own, how do you think they would treat you? When there are no treaties to dictate their behavior, are they inclined to be hospitable? No, they are not."

Rising Hawk scowled into the fire. No one had been openly critical of Gideon in his hearing before. He often said these things to his brother himself, but it angered him when someone else said them.

"You do not have to marry Sassafras," his uncle conceded, "though I think she is a very good girl. There are other women, and you haven't seen even twenty winters yet."

"Tell my grandmother that I am not ready to marry and that if Sassafras's grandmother sends bride bread to her, she should not taste it and should not send any venison in return. It will save everybody a lot of trouble."

"This news will not make your mother or grandmother very happy," his uncle said. "And it troubles me, Rising Hawk. You are not as experienced in these matters as you think. Affection for a woman can grow before you are aware of it. And this white girl, she has no mother here and no clan."

"You have not listened to me, Uncle." Rising Hawk's voice shook with exasperation. "This child is not in my heart. She really is a child, and usually a bad one."

"Well, I know what the village says, and what my eyes have seen."

"Uncle, if you wish to go, they probably need new players for the peach-stone game." Not wanting to be rude, Rising Hawk hastened to add, "I will think about everything you have said, but I will not marry anyone yet." He looked up at his uncle. "And if you must know, this girl has had a vision. She will never marry me . . . or any other man. You may tell my mother so, in confidence, Uncle."

Stands Ready nodded, and knocked his pipe out against a hearthstone. He rose and walked toward the door. Young men were confused these days. It was understandable, of course. With the Confederacy broken, families were living in smaller and smaller houses, and uncles were losing their influence. But now children were taking it into their heads to decide who they would marry, and when. It was a bad change, like so many others nowadays.

There was a huge crowd for Livy's first spinning demonstration. She assumed it was due to the festival. Everyone was still in a holiday mood, and she provided a chance for more gatherings and entertainment. Runs Faster knew better. The gossips had been suggesting that Livy was using love magic, either her own or with help from someone in the village. How else to explain how a handsome young man like Rising Hawk would become infatuated with such a measly, little girl? She had no grace, no spirit, and though pleasant looking, was not pretty. Decidedly not pretty. There had to be something else at the bottom of it, and several in the crowd were sure they knew what it was. Witches were not to be tolerated.

Stands Ready reported the gist of his conversation with Rising Hawk to Buffalo Creek Woman and told her to desist in pestering the young man. He said that Rising Hawk swore he had no intentions toward Livy, and that even if he had, the girl herself had vowed never to marry. At any rate, he was sick of the whole business and suggested that his sister keep her difficulties with her younger son to herself.

She could be content with that. Perhaps Rising Hawk really did look on Gideon's bondgirl as an amusement, a novelty and nothing else. Livy had certainly done nothing to suggest a flirtatious nature. She seemed, in fact, to be entirely without female charm. And it cheered Buffalo Creek Woman to learn of Livy's vision and her vow. Even the spirits were on her side in this.

"Sisters, friends, and relatives," she said with a pleasant smile as she made her welcoming remarks. "We thank you for coming to witness this spinning. We have seen white women engaging in this activity for many years and found it interesting, but we have always had an abundance of trader's cloth for our use. Now this girl has agreed to show us how to spin and later to weave. In the time to come, it may be useful to us. Perhaps someday the traders will want to buy our cloth as they once bought pelts. I do not know. That is why I invited you here, so we could decide for ourselves if this is something we will want to do." She nodded at Livy—who, having lost Rising Hawk as her translator, had no idea what had been said—and motioned for her to begin.

Livy set the distaff and stepped on the treadle. As the wheel began to whirl, she remained standing so that her hands were visible to the crowd. As she spun, Buffalo Creek Woman passed around a full spool of thread and a bit of linen for the women to inspect. A few of them were doubtful. Wasn't there a great deal of work involved to turn this narrow string into cloth? Others wanted to know where they would acquire wheels. Some began to speculate on the possibility of working on such a thing within a mutual aid society. Perhaps in their work groups they could create a great deal of this stuff and sell it to settlers.

Buffalo Creek Woman was beginning to feel very pleased with the result of the demonstration. Several women had left their seats to gather around Livy and observe at close range. Then, from the center of the seated women, there came a low moan. Sassafras had doubled over, as if from some hurt. Her grandmother, who had joined the group around Livy, scurried over to her, full of concern.

Sassafras moaned some more, and this time was loud enough to disrupt the proceedings. She was obviously in severe pain. Livy stopped as the women surrounding her turned to look. Several hurried to the stricken girl's side. Her grandmother was holding Sassafras's head in her lap and speaking urgently to the crowd. What she was saying caused heads to turn back to Livy, and the chatter of the women ceased. Buffalo Creek Woman, her face creased by a frown, pushed her way through the crowd and knelt at the grandmother's side. There were words between them, Buffalo Creek

Woman sounding soothing, the grandmother responding with anger and grief. It ended when the women lifted Sassafras and carried her away. Buffalo Creek Woman's daughter Pretty Girl was one of those supporting the girl.

Runs Faster seized Livy's hand and drew her up. Speaking rapidly, she motioned for Livy to go inside while she sprinted away to find Rising Hawk. He would be needed to explain the situation to Livy, and quickly. When accusations of witchcraft flew, decisions regarding guilt or innocence were sometimes made by the victim's family within hours. The accused might be confronted, judged, and executed within the same day. Sassafras's grandmother had wasted no time in pointing the finger of suspicion at Livy.

Chapter 20

Mr. Wilkes was surprised to see the delegation from the road crew. He was even more surprised to see the Pelton boy, looking as miserable as a thief on the way to the gallows, among them. It had been five months since he had disposed of those two youngsters, and he had heard nothing of them until Gideon had come to the village recently to recover that flax wheel for the little girl. According to Gideon's rather terse account, the youngsters were adjusting well to his family; the girl, in particular, was proving to be invaluable and the boy, after a rough start, was settling down.

Ephraim was brought forward to stand before Mr. Wilkes, while Lawson, casting black looks at him, was called upon to give his account of the boy's tale about the Seneca party at Gunn's homestead. Eph's bow was produced as evidence. Mr. Wilkes, seated at his desk, considered the man's story, taking in his appearance and demeanor. Then he spoke to Ephraim.

"You have heard Mr. Lawson speak. Is what he has said about the Gunn household true?"

Ephraim, unable to look Mr. Wilkes in the eye, simply shrugged his shoulders.

"I have asked you a question and expect to be answered civilly."

Ephraim, at a loss as to how to proceed, put his hands in his jacket pockets. If he could minimize the damage he may already have done to Gideon, he meant to do it, but he needed time to think. The room was too hot. He wished someone would open a window. He stood silent.

The foreman, Samuel Knox, stepped forward.

"Mr. Wilkes, I have two other men on my crew who heard the boy. We also have the boy's things. Besides that bow and a couple of arrows, he had a blanket, a knife, a tinderbox, and a few other items for his comfort that seem to indicate he was up to more than resetting traps. The word of my crew ought to be sufficient against a bondboy who's obviously a runaway."

Mr. Wilkes nodded and cleared his throat. "If that is the case, then I must agree with you. Now you, sir." He put his hand out and shook Ephraim by the shoulder, making him wince. "Take your hands out of your pockets, your eyes off the floor, and answer me."

Ephraim took his hands out of his pockets and very slowly brought his eyes level with Wilkes's. That gentleman was pleased to see the boy's discomfort. At least he was aware of the inappropriateness of his behavior. It seemed the devil hadn't made a total conquest of the wretch.

"Were you, as Mr. Knox here has suggested, running away? And this time, I would appreciate a reply."

Ephraim's voice was low, but he answered. "Yes, sir."

Mr. Wilkes looked around at the party with some satisfaction. He knew how to deal with recalcitrant boys. "Are you aware that by removing yourself from your master's control, you have not only broken your contract but stolen your labor from him? That labor is how you pay for your room and board. Have you no sense of obligation?"

"I was meaning to come back, sir. I was only going visiting." At this the men broke into derisive laughter. Mr. Wilkes waited for it to die down.

"And are you the owner of the items in this bundle?"

Ephraim hesitated.

"I asked you a question," Wilkes said.

"Not exactly. I borrowed them." There was more snickering at this.

"You stole them. I thought as much."

"No, sir. I would have brought them back."

Mr. Wilkes looked aggrieved at this. "Can it be you really do not know the difference between borrowing and thieving? I am afraid someone has been remiss in your education." He paused to let the weight of his disapproval sink in.

Eph stared at his feet and wondered if Mr. Wilkes would mind if he sat on the floor for a while. He was awfully tired.

When Mr. Wilkes judged the boy had experienced enough humiliation, he continued. "Ultimately, we must blame the adults who have had charge of you. Fortunately, you are young enough to be influenced for the better." He turned to Mr. Knox. "I can deal with the boy, sir, but what assistance do you expect on this other matter?"

"I want assurances from this Gideon Gunn that these Seneca parties keep off. They sold this land to Phelps and Gorham in eighty-eight. With the Shawnee, Delaware, and Miami raising hell west of here, we got a right to be nervous. And we've had our share of trouble along the Genesee now and again, too. Every time settlers come in contact with those savages, someone gets hurt. I'm not going to expose my crew to that kind of danger. Wolves, bears, and swamp fever are bad enough."

"You'll need to talk to the town council about this," Mr. Wilkes replied. "I have no authority to act alone on this matter. But I think you'll find the town in agreement with you. We've suspected for a long time that there was something not quite right with that household. No one knows for sure where their loyalties lie. I expect there are more than a few people who would like to see that gentleman homesteading in some other locality."

Knox shifted his weight and put a hand to his chin.

"If it comes to that, my crew and I can help you out."

Another voice called out, "We'll help this Gunn fellow out on a rail." There was laughter and applause at that.

Mr. Wilkes looked concerned. "I doubt that it will come to that," he said.

"Do you?" Knox asked, unconvinced. "Well, I hope you're right."

Ephraim, minus all his plunder but the blanket, was escorted unceremoniously down to the cellar. Mrs. Wilkes expressed her opinion that he should be whipped as a runaway and delivered up to the sheriff at Canandaigua without delay. Then she promised him that if he should so much as lay a finger on her larder, she would do it herself.

Ephraim simply rolled up in the blanket and tried to sleep. His head was aching and he felt feverish. Food was the furthest thing from his mind, though a little cool water would be nice right now. But his real concern was how he could slip away and warn Polly and Gideon. He was tortured with thoughts of how his blundering would look to them like a betrayal. If Mr. Knox had his way, a delegation from the village, perhaps even a mob, could be on their doorstep by noon tomorrow. And of course they'd blame him. His name would come up first thing, and they'd suspect he'd gone directly to the village on purpose. They'd hate him forever. He had tossed and turned for an hour when it came to him that the house was quiet and he ought to climb the steps and try the door.

Before he could so much as sit up, the heavy footsteps of three or four men sounded above him. There was the click of the bolt being lifted, and the door swung open, bringing in some light and Mr. Wilkes's voice.

"There he is, Mr. Gunther. I cannot, I am sorry to say, vouch for either his industry or his honesty, but if you are willing, as you say, to take him on and make a God-fearing citizen of him, then the village will be grateful to you. Frankly, sir, I believe he is redeemable, or I would not inflict him on your household."

It was too dark in the cellar, and the light from above was too bright, for Ephraim to make out the man's features. He got to his feet slowly.

"Come up here," Mr. Wilkes commanded. Ephraim picked up the blanket and reluctantly went up the stairs. If there had been even the slightest chance of gaining the door, he would have taken it. But there wasn't. There were three of them: his new master—a tall, sturdily built German farmer—and two younger men, whom Eph took to be the farmer's sons. He had never seen men that big before.

The older man, Herr Gunther, took hold of him by his upper arms and lifted him into the room. He looked disdainfully at Eph's size and said something to his sons, in German, that made them laugh. Ephraim was simply too ill and miserable to take offense. All he wanted to do was lie down. He longed for the quiet cellar.

The proceedings were concluded quickly. Mr. Wilkes simply said that the boy's previous situation had proved unsatisfactory. The village wanted him off its hands as soon as possible and was willing to pay a generous sum to board the boy through the coming year. A very generous sum.

That was that. Ephraim found himself wedged between the two sons, escorted to the back of a wagon, and unceremoniously dumped in.

Chapter 21

Runs Faster found Rising Hawk on the riverbank with two friends. She burst in upon the group without explanation and alarmed them all by seizing Rising Hawk by the arm and begging him to follow her. "What is it?" the young men asked in chorus. With the power of the Iroquois Confederacy broken by the American war, and the western tribes turned contemptuous of the Seneca's efforts to be neutral, everyone was nervous. Alarm such as this could mean anything.

"It is nothing—nothing you need be concerned about," Runs Faster cried out. "This only concerns us." The two friends sat back, only half convinced by Rising Hawk's crazy sister. Her eyes were wide with fright.

"What is it?" Rising Hawk repeated. "Why are you running? Is it our grandmother?" His voice held concern, not panic. He had caused Grandmother some difficulty lately. He hoped she had not taken ill with vexation.

Runs Faster was breathing hard from her flight. She had had to ask at two longhouses at opposite sides of the village before finding him. Why was he asking questions now? When every moment brought disaster closer to Livy? She drew a deep breath to calm herself.

"Sassafras took ill when Livy was showing us the spinning wheel. People have been talking"—she lowered her voice to a whisper—"about love magic. Sassafras's grandmother accused Livy of poisoning her."

It took time for it to sink in. Rising Hawk's face changed as he realized the situation. "They suspect witchcraft?"

His two friends drew closer. This was a serious and deadly accusation. Could the girl be a witch? Well . . . maybe. There were signs. Hadn't Rising Hawk been teaching her to hunt? The first thing one noticed about a witch was her unfeminine behavior. And if Rising Hawk was as indifferent toward the girl as he claimed, why couldn't he stop talking about her? Politeness kept them from pointing out the obvious, but she was a rather ordinary girl. Sorcery could be at work here. It was not the first time an outsider had been accused of such a thing.

Rising Hawk didn't wait to discuss the matter with his friends, but they went with him anyway. If there was sorcery and danger, they intended to protect him—from himself, if necessary. He took off at a run, leaving Runs Faster trailing behind.

He found Livy in the longhouse, huddled far back on a sleeping platform with the curtain down. When she saw it was Rising Hawk who had drawn the curtain, she crawled out to sit on the edge of the platform. She was baffled. The women outside had seemed frightened of her and angry.

Rising Hawk leaned over and put his hands on her shoulders. "Livy, listen very carefully to me. When you were showing the spinning wheel to the women, did you make any strange motions? Did you blow anything into the air or look at Sassafras at any time?"

"No. And I didn't even know Sassafras was there until she moaned. She sounded awful, Rising Hawk. She was in terrible pain." She looked up at him. "What do they say I did? Have I broken some kind of rule? If I have, I didn't mean to. You know that." Her eyes were clear. She didn't look the least bit guilty.

"They think you have put a spell on Sassafras."

Livy didn't know whether to laugh or cry. For the first time she noticed the two young men who had followed Rising Hawk into the house. It helped to see the seriousness of their expressions. She did not laugh.

"I am not a witch, Rising Hawk. I don't even believe in such things. It's ridiculous." If she had expected Rising Hawk to agree with her, she was disappointed.

"I believe you," he whispered, patting her shoulder slightly, then turning away. "But someone is responsible. They will be looking."

Buffalo Creek Woman left her second daughter to help with Sassafras. She could see that her own presence was already suspect. She was the one, after all, who had brought the girl among them. But Pretty Girl was sweet and unobtrusive, with quiet eyes that took in everything. No one would object to her being there, and it was essential that everything be observed. Buffalo Creek Woman had no doubt that witches caused illness and death, but it had also been her experience that sometimes accusations had more to do with old grievances than real evidence. Between Sassafras's grandmother and Rising Hawk's, there had recently been unpleasantness over this marriage business. One had to protect oneself from misguided accusations.

Rising Hawk was already in the longhouse, whispering with his father, Cold Keeper. Buffalo Creek Woman saw with displeasure that his two friends, the Onondaga boy Shadow, and Dream Teller, her brother's son, were with him. She would have preferred a private discussion. Something must be done with the girl and quickly, before things got out of hand and a council was called. Once a formal inquiry was started, anything might happen. There could well be a verdict. And then would the girl have enough sense to confess if it came to that? A confession from a convicted witch could mean atonement and life. A denial brought death almost certainly. She was afraid the child was too ignorant to be sensible. Despite the desperate situation, she had the presence of mind to act as if nothing much was wrong.

"Husband," she said quietly, "will you ask my brother to come? Tell him it concerns Rising Hawk."

Stands Ready heard and followed his brother-in-law without a word. It was all over the village. A crowd of women were gathered at the longhouse where Sassafras lay, and there were already suggestions being put forward that the white girl should at least be restrained somewhere. That might calm people down a little. He had also heard that Sassafras had bled. Where or how much was not known yet, but it raised the possibility that the foolish girl, humiliated over Rising Hawk's rejection of her, had eaten a poison root. There were sometimes suicides over matters more trivial. But had it been the usual poison, *o' no'h see*, she would have died quickly, in the time it took a snake to swallow a toad. Whatever the cause, poison or witchcraft, the sachems were sure to hold an investigation.

"We should talk to the sachems, before the girl's family has an opportunity," he advised. "If there is no evidence of witchcraft, we can perhaps persuade them that the white fathers would be very displeased to hear of the death of such a young girl at the hands of the Seneca."

Cold Keeper shrugged. "Perhaps—" He was interrupted by his son.

"There has been no talk of killing, Uncle. She has done nothing that they can prove. Why do you talk of such things? Don't be so stupid."

His elders were stunned into silence. They would get no rational assistance from Rising Hawk, they could see that. Buffalo Creek Woman turned to her brother and husband.

"We shall take the child to the sachems for protection. Once the matter has been looked into, everyone will see that this girl could not possibly be a witch. She is ignorant of such things. They should look elsewhere for the witch, or wizard. Have they even considered that perhaps there is a jealous man involved? Sassafras is a very pretty girl and has had lovers before. It could just as likely be a man." Buffalo Creek Woman had every confidence in her explanation. It was undoubtedly some rejected lover.

Cold Keeper was keenly aware of his younger son's growing attachment to the white girl. He marveled that a male and female should find as much to talk about as these two did. At any rate, it would be prudent to send her away. It seemed to him the only safe course of action.

His son sat scowling at them all. He had one arm around the child in an unseemly, protective embrace. She was looking from one speaker to another as if she could follow the discourse. Clearly frightened by Rising Hawk's outburst, her face was paler than usual. There is not much to her, Cold Keeper thought, as he always did when he contemplated the riddle of his son's attachment. No wonder people are suspicious.

He smiled kindly at Livy and spoke to his son. "Take some parched corn and some blankets and leave now," he said. "Take her back to your brother. This problem will come to its own conclusion in time. But it would be wise to take her out of here."

"No!" Buffalo Creek Woman cried. "If they leave, it will be the rabbit running before the dog. Someone will want to give chase. If she is here in the village, we can protect her. If they are alone on the trail, any warrior could hunt them down. It is a dangerous and foolish idea."

Rising Hawk rose to his feet. "My father is right. We will leave," he said firmly.

Before he could say anything else, Shadow and Dream Teller grabbed his arms. Shocked, he tried to shake them off, but the two friends tightened their grip.

"No," Shadow said. "She is working magic on you, that you should think so foolishly. Stay."

Shadow spoke gently to his friend, but Rising Hawk was enraged. He yanked them forward, scattering kettles and kindling as the three of them fell to the ground. His mother screamed. The older men caught Shadow and tried to pull him away. Runs Faster darted to her aunt's fire to be well out of the way. But Livy, conscious of nothing but Rising Hawk, waded into the fight before she knew what she was doing.

She crouched and grabbed a piece of kindling just as a moccasined foot shot from the thrashing pile and smacked her in the ribs. With a grunt, she fell against the platform. The blow knocked the breath out of her, but she held on to the stick and dragged herself upright.

Shadow struggled between the older men, arguing furiously,

but Dream Teller was on top of Rising Hawk, pinning him to the floor. Without thinking, Livy threw the wood with all her strength at the back of his head. There was a thud and a groan, and she jumped on him, pulling his shoulders.

He rolled, smothering her beneath him. Something hit her face and she tasted blood. Then Dream Teller was yanked to his feet, and Livy was dragged across the floor. Someone had taken her ankle and was trying to pull her from the tangle. She kicked and heard Buffalo Creek Woman cry out in pain. At the sound, the scuffle ceased.

The older men were holding Shadow and Dream Teller. Shadow had a trickle of blood running from a gash over his eye and Dream Teller, glaring darkly at Livy, had a bloody head.

Rising Hawk's clothes were torn and his knuckles bloodied. As he struggled to rise to a sitting position, he saw Livy dazed and breathing hard, getting slowly to her knees.

She had a red welt below her eye that would soon darken. A thin stream of blood had run from the corner of her mouth and down her chin into the neck of her gown. Her face was mired with ashes and there were rivulets of blood between her white teeth. Looking around, she caught his eye and smiled defiantly. She looked as if she had just tasted the living heart of her enemy.

Buffalo Creek Woman stood over her, holding her own wrist tight against her body and lecturing Livy with harsh words. "I should take you to the river right now and plunge you under. Have you any manners at all? Fighting with men like that? And my wrist! I can't feel it. You have broken it!"

Shadow looked over at Livy, who was still furious and not at all contrite, and said sullenly, "She is very unwomanly. She fights like a boy . . . a *white* boy."

Stands Ready tightened his grip on Dream Teller and suddenly laughed out loud. "I am surprised to see she has such a strong arm. You would not know it to look at her. We must call her Throws Her Firewood or, possibly, Mankiller. My son's head has a lump on it the size of an apple."

Rising Hawk said nothing. Still breathing hard, he crossed to his mother and examined her wrist. It was not broken. His sister came and drew her mother away.

Rising Hawk reached into an upper platform and pulled out a hunter's pouch of parched corn. He tore blankets from the beds, took pouches of powder and shot, and motioned to Livy to pick up his gun. Then they were gone.

Chapter 22

Polly peeled the damp cattail fluff from baby Samuel's bottom and dropped it into the fireplace. A sour smell rose briefly from the ashes. She tucked a fistful of new stuff into his cradle board. Hastily she wiped her hands on her apron and went back to kneading biscuit dough.

Her gloom and melancholy of two days ago had vanished. Most of the early corn harvest was in. They had less than an acre to finish. John and Gideon and her two older ones were in the field now, waiting on her for their dinner. She had left the four of them dozing in the shade of a maple like a heap of dusty and disheveled puppies.

Ephraim had run off, and they felt his loss in the field, but Gideon had picked up his trail easily enough. It looked as if he had gone right to the road crew. Whether he had planned to join up or just follow the road to town didn't matter, Gideon said. He would find the boy when they were finished. He wouldn't waste valuable harvest weather on him. Ephraim had caused enough trouble for one season as it was.

Gideon had laughed about it. He had sat down on the porch and laughed till tears came into his eyes. "I was swindled," he said when she'd asked him what had come over him. "I got myself a miniature of John Gage, that's all. And just like old John, I can guarantee you right now that nobody in the township is going to want him. We'll have him back in a week. They'll be begging me to take him away."

When Polly caught sight of the men coming up her walkway, that's exactly what came to mind at first. But what could they have to do with Ephraim? She counted a dozen men at least and she only recognized the two, Mr. Wilkes and the mayor, Luther Borst. The sight of Mr. Wilkes calmed her. He was a bit sanctimonious, but he was accounted a good man.

She picked up Samuel and went to the open door. Even in her plain tow frock with her sunbonnet hanging down her back, she was lovely. It was almost as if she were playing at being a farmer's wife, and her silk gowns were airing by the hearth.

"Are you looking for my husband, Mr. Wilkes?"

"We are."

"He's not here. What is it you want?"

"We ain't here to talk to you, ma'am. We're here on man's business," came a rough voice from the back of the crowd. It was one of the workmen, stomping on her violets.

"Then I expect you've made the trip for nothing. Good day." She turned to go in.

Mr. Wilkes and Mayor Borst stepped onto the porch. Wilkes put a restraining hand on her sleeve. "Please find him, Mrs. Gunn. I've no influence. Some of them are drunk. He's safer here than in the open."

"It's all right. I'm here," Gideon said softly, emerging from the bedroom. "I didn't like the look of that meeting out front, so I used the window." He smiled uneasily at the two men. "Now what's going on? You catch my boy?" Their faces were grim. "Who'd he kill, Luther? I hope you don't aim to hang the brat."

There was a commotion at the doorway. Mr. Knox and two of his crew pushed past Wilkes and Borst and nearly knocked Polly over in their haste to take Gideon's Kentucky rifle from its rack. Gideon moved slightly to shield Polly and the baby.

Knox spoke to Gideon. "That boy of yours said you've got Indians coming and going here."

Gideon's dark eyes appraised him. "I don't believe I know you." He turned to Wilkes. "What's this about Ephraim?"

"He said you have large parties of Seneca coming to your land."

"Depends what you call 'large.' Ephraim exaggerates," Gideon said mildly.

Mr. Wilkes cleared his throat. "It's true then."

"Yes, but I don't see why it's your concern."

"The road crew wants your assurance that they aren't coming back," Mr. Wilkes announced. Then he leaned forward and lowered his voice. "I've talked with them, Gideon. They have scores to settle." Gideon could feel Polly at his back, breathless and listening.

"There's no danger," Gideon said. "It was only my mother and father and a few cousins. They were scouting the deer herd, wondering if it would be worth hunting this far east anymore. They decided against it. The nation's big winter hunt will be west of the Genesee, and my folks won't be back until next year. By then this little sewing circle will be done with the road. Will that help your boys sleep better at night?" he said to Knox.

"You don't look like a half-breed."

"I never said I was."

"If I lived here, Wilkes, and had family to protect, I would want to know what this fellow did during the war, since the Seneca sided with the British. Then I might have to insist on knowing just where his loyalties lie now."

"You don't live here," Gideon said, "and that's a lot of insisting for a stranger. But even if you were a neighbor, I'd tell you that the war's been over for ten years, and it's none of your business. I've broken no laws."

"Gideon," Mayor Borst interrupted, "I want to know."

"You just had my answer, Luther."

"So you've got Seneca family and they come on social calls?"

"Yes, and they like to look things over. It's their land, too, Luther. I bought it from the Phelps and Gorham Land Company in eighty-nine with their money, mostly. Some of the money was mine from trapping, but most of it came from cashing in the trade goods and cattle and such the government handed out to my family over the years. They thought it was a pretty good joke at the time. I own one-third. My parents and my uncle own the rest. I won't tell them they can't use their land."

"I know something of the law," Mr. Wilkes interrupted, "and the law says Indians can't engage in land transactions without the involvement of the federal government. You are violating the Indian Trade and Intercourse Act."

"The law says they can't sell their land," Gideon said. "It doesn't say anything about buying it back."

"You're subverting the law's intent," Mr. Wilkes said sourly, "bringing a pack of Seneca back into the township, just when we've gotten rid of them."

"That's not the law's intent; it's yours."

The baby began to fuss for his dinner. As Polly moved toward the bedroom, Lawson caught her arm and stopped her.

Gideon lunged. Two of Knox's men blocked and held him. "Don't get excited," Knox said. "No disrespect to your wife, Gunn. We just don't want the woman to come back with another rifle is all."

"I don't have another rifle. Now let her go, and get out!"

Lawson looked at Knox, who nodded. He dropped Polly's arm, but stayed close by, leering at her and blocking her exit.

"We're going," Knox said, "but we still want to know where you spent the war and whom you served under."

"Canada, and no one."

"I lost my whole family at Cherry Valley, Gunn," Lawson said quietly. "That's real amusing."

"It's the truth."

"He's not alone," Knox said. "Aikens there lost two brothers at Canajoharie. Vroman lost his father and uncles at Schoharie. Most of the men on my crew were hurt one way or the other on the frontier, by your Iroquois."

"Not by me," Gideon said, looking at Lawson. "Before I even thought about getting into it, I was shot by American militia. I was thirteen and careless, and they were overanxious. Thanks to a party of Mohawks—who were their real target, it turned out—I didn't die. I spent four years, six months of it flat on my back, as the guest of Father Henry Clairemont of the Anglican Society for Propagating the Gospel."

"You can't get any more Tory than that," Knox said. "My guess is you slipped back and forth over the border, passed for American, and spied for Joseph Brant."

Gideon started to laugh. "A spy? I couldn't even speak English, Knox. I wouldn't have been very convincing. I did see Joseph Brant once, though, from a distance at one of the big councils."

"Been to any other big councils lately?" A lanky boy with sandy hair pushed his way into the room. He came within three feet of Gideon and stood looking closely at his face. Gideon glanced quickly at Polly. The boy continued, "I was took prisoner in Kentucky by a band of Shawnee. This year in late February, about a month before the British at Detroit bought me and set me free, my Shawnee master took me to a council. The Americans had sent a message to the western tribes saying they wanted a peace council. The Americans even said they would honor a cease-fire. But the tribes refused. Unless the Americans agreed to the Indian boundary line in Ohio, there would be no peace council. So the tribes needed someone to write a letter to the Americans, listing their demands. At the same time they wanted Lieutenant Governor Simcoe in Upper Canada to know exactly what the Americans were up to. They expected the British to help them—to supply them with ammunition and food.

"My master thought I could write both letters, but I'd be damned if I was going to help the western tribes get help from the British. I know enough to scratch out a simple message, but I flat out told him I couldn't read or write, let alone understand Indian well enough to do it right. He was disappointed and bashed me around a little, but he believed me. Then the Seneca pushed this fella forward. He said a few words to the Shawnee and Miami chiefs, then sat down and wrote messages to the American secretary of war and Simcoe.

"It took a long time. He was careful, asking over and over again if this was what they wanted. I had a good long time to watch him, and I'm willing to swear on the Bible that it was this fella here."

Gideon looked the boy in the eye. "It wasn't me. You've misremembered."

"This young man says the council was in late February, Gideon," Mr. Wilkes said. "You stopped at the pauper's auction in late March. That gave you three weeks to make the trip east from Ohio. When I saw you, it was obvious you hadn't been home for a long while."

"Can you account for your time then?" Knox asked.

"I was hunting and helping a friend with his traps. I'd be a damn fool to go hunting all the way to Ohio, now wouldn't I?"

The room was still. Someone cleared his throat.

"It couldn't possibly have been my husband, Mr. Wilkes," Polly said. "You and everyone else around here know Gideon can't read or write."

Mr. Wilkes stood looking at the floor; then he nodded vigorously and said with some excitement, "Of course he can't. He signed the children's contracts with an X. I'd forgotten that."

"The truth is, no matter how diligently Father Clairemont tried, the most he was able to teach Gideon to read was a few passages of the Bible. Actually"—at this point Polly blushed before continuing—"he'd only memorized them. Gideon used to pore over that Bible to please Father Clairemont, but it was hopeless as you know, Mr. Wilkes."

There was a slight pause before Knox said, "Then these books ma'am"—he indicated the Bible, a book of sermons, and an almanac on the mantle— "belong to you?"

Polly nodded. "All except the Bible. That belongs to my husband. It was a gift from Father Clairemont. He treasures it."

Knox looked at Gideon again. "Yes, we had you figured for a real Bible lover. The Seneca are known for it."

In the long silence that followed, Polly was aware of Lawson drumming on Gideon's rifle with his clawlike nails.

At Gideon's request, Mr. Wilkes lingered after the others cleared out. Gideon picked up his rifle and sat at the table, loading powder and shot, his face a tight-lipped mask. Polly went quietly into the bedroom to nurse Samuel. It was his crying that had finally ended the stalemate.

John Gage appeared at the door, holding Hannah and Henry by their hands. "Oh," he said, eyeing Mr. Wilkes. "I thought they'd all gone."

"Just about, John," Gideon said, laying his rifle aside. "Wilkes, about my runaway boy. I want him back. No one else will put up with him anyway; he ain't worth spit. If he's cost you anything, I'll pay."

Wilkes didn't bother to explain about the Gunthers. The whole incident had left a sour taste in his mouth. He wanted to get as far away from Gideon as possible. "I'll see what I can do," Mr. Wilkes said, and made his retreat.

Chapter 23

Gideon watched Wilkes disappear into the woods. "They're gone . . . for now," he said.

Polly came back from putting the baby down and handed some apples to the children, who were seated at the table. From the flush in her cheeks, Gideon could see she was angry. He hoped it was directed at that ruffian Lawson who had taken such a shine to her, and not at him.

John was quietly getting his belongings together. He tied a bundle and reached for his rifle.

"Check for lookouts," Gideon said. "Then move the livestock. We can tether the cow and oxen, but we'll have to pen the sheep and pigs inside the longhouse with us."

Polly looked questioningly at Gideon, then at the children. Hannah bit into her apple, then took the chunk out of her mouth to examine it. Henry sat with both hands on the table, clutching his apple. He rested his chin on it and looked up, first at John collecting his things, then at his parents.

"It's just a precaution, sweetheart. They won't try anything by daylight, not that sort. But they'll be bolder after dark." Gideon squatted on the hearth and began collecting the heavier pots and kettles. "I'll take these up for you, Polly. You bring the babies."

She didn't move. The flush in her cheeks deepened.

"Please, Polly. If you want to brain me with a fire iron later, I'll lie down and let you."

He crawled out of the ashes and took her hands in his. "I promise you," he said, "nobody is going to get hurt. They're a pack of cowards."

She yanked her hands away. "We both know there's nothing more dangerous." Polly glanced at the children, then lowered her voice. "You didn't tell me about the council last February. You said you were hunting. You said the game was scarce, so you had to go farther than you'd planned. And that story about seeing John Gage and helping him with his traps; was that a lie, too?"

"I judged it would be safer all round if I left you out of it."

"Why did you go?"

"Cornplanter asked me to. The western tribes have been using Simon Girty to translate. He's never been interested in peace with the Americans. They suspect he hasn't always been faithful in his translations. I had to, Pol. Cornplanter rarely asks anything of me, and I owe him."

"Did you see that boy at the council?"

"Yes. I knew him the minute he spoke up. That was a smooth lie you told, Polly. It convinced Wilkes, and the people in Vienna will believe it. They've stayed clear of us and have no reason to suspect I'm any kind of scholar. But the road crew will believe that boy."

"Wouldn't the letters that you wrote be looked on as a service to the Americans?"

"Those letters were hostile. The one to the Canadian lieutenant governor contained the whole text of the American secretary's letter. The American government wants to keep the British out of this. They won't appreciate my interference."

"Gideon, what have you done?"

"Not now, Polly."

"Gideon, those men could take it into their heads to hang you," she whispered, and sank to her knees beside him.

Even Hannah stopped eating when Papa kissed Mama and got ashes and soot all over her. Solemnly, Henry handed his apple, still untouched, to Hannah and left the table. Without a word he began gathering their playthings together.

"Polly, listen. The smartest thing I learned from the Seneca about fighting is that when you're outnumbered, don't be a fool. We'll stay out of their way. No house or barn is worth anyone getting hurt over. I don't intend to do anything foolish." He kissed her again and whispered, "Don't get into a temper now. The children are going to get all riled up if you do."

"Better a temper than a fainting fit," John Gage said, standing over them, cradling his rifle. "Now, if you two don't mind, I could do with a little help. Those sheep don't herd themselves."

After dark, John and Gideon returned to the homestead to keep watch over the trail.

"I counted twelve, plus Knox," Gideon whispered. "There's no danger of them finding the longhouse, John. Judging from the way they're cracking their heads on tree limbs, I'd say most of them are blind drunk."

John peered into the darkness. "You can't see at night no more, boy. I tell you there's sixteen."

They were on their knees, just beyond the circle of light cast by the burning barn. The mob had disappeared into the cabin. At Knox's direction they had searched the dark woods for a hiding hole, expecting to find the family huddled underground. When half an hour of furious looking produced nothing, they'd given up.

The cabin glowed like a punched-tin lantern, beams of light escaping from every chink and window. A torch was hurled into the air, up into the loft, where the children had slept. There was laughter and cheering.

Gideon watched impassively. The making of the house and barn had been backbreaking labor, and his pride and joy, but there was no help for it.

John patted his shoulder. "Let's go. You don't need to see any more. Polly and the children are safe."

Gideon nodded, hesitating just long enough for one last look. He heard John cross the creek, and turned to go.

He started running before his mind had fully comprehended the image. Four men, standing between him and the creek, one of them swinging a club, and the night exploding into stars.

They pulled him into the light of the burning barn. The man with the club stuck his hand under Gideon's nose and felt his faint breath. Two of the men had chased John into the cornfield and tackled him. The three of them were rolling around and cursing and landing blows indiscriminately.

"He dead?" Lawson asked, kneeling by Gideon's body.

"Naw."

Lawson grinned, then moved Gideon's arms to his side and straddled him.

"Hold his legs," he ordered his companion. "He's gonna kick like a mule."

He grabbed hold of Gideon's bloodied ear and pulled. Gideon came to with a groan.

"Good," Lawson said, yanking again. "It just ain't the same 'less the man's awake and can see it coming."

He released Gideon's ear and smiled at him. "The Shawnee got this trick of paring a man's ear like an apple skin, till it hangs down to his shoulder, like baby's curls. You familiar with that?"

Gideon began to struggle. The man sitting on his legs laughed and clamped down. Lawson pushed Gideon's bloodied head into the dirt and held it there.

"It's a neat trick," Lawson continued. "But paring an ear requires a knife, and I don't favor a knife. It ain't near as satisfying as using your bare hands." He held up his right hand, brandishing the long nails on his thumb and forefinger. "Now these are real effective when applied to a man's eyeball. By the by, no one believed your missus."

John heard the cry, low and suppressed, then rising into a shriek. It was over by the time Knox came to investigate. By then Lawson had tossed something small and bloody into the fire and had disappeared into the darkness.

John wept with relief. Gideon was mangled, but alive. By the light of the burning barn, he cauterized the wounds and bound them with his own shirt. Then he sat with him through the night, lying on top of him toward morning when the fire went down and the cold began to be a misery to them both.

Gideon shook violently and drifted in and out. When he could speak, he begged John to leave him for an hour, so Polly could know he was alive and not have to grieve through the night.

"It won't kill her," John said. "All this blood might attract a bear or some big cat. She'd rather grieve for one night than find chewed pieces of you dangling from the crook of a panther tree."

Polly came at first light, pale and rumpled, toting blankets, and fell on Gideon with the fierceness of a she-bear. John let little Henry help cut boughs from a white pine. They used the boughs to fashion a bed under the tree and kept Gideon there, nearly motionless for a day.

The children were devastated. Most of Papa's face was hidden by bandages. He lay still and quiet, but when the pain was at its worst, his toes wriggled, flexing up, then down, for hours. Polly allowed them to soothe themselves by crawling carefully into bed with him and resting their heads on his belly, or holding fast to his hands. By the next morning, John allowed that Gideon might be able to walk home to the longhouse with their assistance, and helped him sit up, his back supported by the tree.

"They didn't gird the orchard," John said dully. His own bruises were hurting bad, and Polly was not supplying him with enough brandy to ease the pain. "I recollect this country after Sullivan went through. The army even girded the trees in the orchards then. This isn't quite as bad, but it's a close approximation."

"It's not so bad," Polly said cheerfully, directing a warning frown at John. She settled herself next to Gideon and took his hand. Yesterday she had resisted the urge to mother him. His pride had been hurt nearly as much as his body, and he had been cool and distant. She wanted him alone so she could throw herself at him and tell him over and over again how grateful she was to have him alive, and that it wasn't his fault, and how lucky they were.

"Gideon, if you want to stay with your folks at Jenuchshadego for a while, I'd be pleased to help you transport the kiddies," John offered.

Gideon was studying the ground. "No. Thanks. But no. I ain't slinking off like some beat dog. I can still sight a rifle. I'll go to

Jenuchshadego in four days, and be back in four more with a war party. If this Knox wants a war, I'll give him one."

Polly gasped. "You can't mean that, Gideon. You said no house or barn was worth anybody getting hurt."

"It ain't. But I was careless and I got hurt. That changes things." She flung his hand down and walked off.

"Eye bothering you?" John said quietly.

"It's not as bad."

"I don't believe you, son. A man would have to be hurtin' bad and out of his mind to believe the Seneca would join in some piddling little matter like this when Cornplanter's trying his damnedest to stay out of the real war in Ohio."

"Rising Hawk and his friends—"

"They aren't as foolish as that. Cornplanter would kill you himself before he'd let you stir things up now. Besides, your mama may dote on you, but if you're expecting the rest of the women to come up with provisions for a war party just because your looks got spoiled, you're going to be disappointed."

"I want that bastard took my eye, John. I got some tricks of my own to show him."

"Don't be ridiculous. In your present condition you couldn't thread a needle, let alone take on that fella." He paused and rubbed at his nose. "I'm sorry, Gideon. I wished I could have saved you, son, but I was outnumbered. Look on the bright side. We're all nearly in one piece. You ain't putrefied, so chances are you ain't likely to die. All they accomplished was to mar your looks and inconvenience you some. I'll stay over this winter and help you rebuild when the mud clears."

"Look at me, John. I'm a goddamn cripple, and I'm wore out."

"You're just sick, son. It'll pass. You still got one good eye and both arms and legs."

Gideon pressed a hand to the bandage and was silent a minute. "Polly's expecting again, John. She'll be laid up in the spring, just when I need her strong."

John's lips moved as he calculated on his fingers. "Good lord, son. You were plowing in the middle of hay making? There ain't a man alive with that kind of energy. It's unnatural." Gideon's head sank down, and he studied the dirt.

"Look, son, would it help if we used the timber the road crew's already cut?"

"Yeah. We can rip up the road and sneak the logs off at night. Shouldn't leave ruts more'n a foot deep. Little Henry can cover our tracks."

"I don't propose to sneak," John said. "I'll go to Vienna to report on this. You may not be too popular around here, but I think they'll have to agree that you're the injured party. I'll suggest Knox make restitution with logs."

Gideon snorted.

"Now, look, son, this is the best advice I got, and I'm startin' to take offense at your attitude. It wasn't the town folk did this. It was a bunch of liquored-up ditchdiggers."

"Who wouldn't have done it if they didn't figure Wilkes and Borst and the rest of them would look the other way."

"You don't know that for a fact, Gideon. You've got to give them a chance to make good. Besides, if they did look the other way, you ain't entirely free from blame."

"What?"

"You been living in the midst of these folk and just pretending they ain't there. They don't know anything about you."

"They know I leave them alone. That should be good enough."

"Should be, but it ain't, and it don't show much understanding of human nature. How long do you suppose the Seneca would tolerate it? Someone like me builds a cabin in a Seneca village, gives no account of himself for five years, and invites Shawnee to come visit on occasion. You don't think the sachems would get nervous?"

Gideon's laugh was bitter. "Probably, but they'd call on you politely and ask you about it in a roundabout way. They wouldn't stand by and let the Mohawk burn you out. But if that happened, they'd expect you to take your revenge."

"They'll hang you, you know. You bring trouble down on these folks, and they'd be right to do it. You needn't go puttin' on that closemouthed Seneca look for me. You know they would, and hell, I'd let 'em. I'd have to stand aside and let 'em do it, no matter how it tore at my heart. People got every right to be skittish about Indians out here, with the western tribes warring in the Ohio and the British up in Canada starting rumors all the time.

"Then what happens to Polly? You'd leave that girl out here alone, with all these children? You're the one been seeding that woman like a love-struck bull moose. You got heavy responsibilities, and you ain't gonna go and leave 'em to me! Not me!" John scowled, pulled out his pipe, and jammed it, unlit, into his mouth. Several minutes passed in stony silence while Gideon picked at his shirtsleeve.

"I do believe," Gideon whispered finally, "that even burned over, this is one of the prettiest spots for a homestead I've ever seen."

John was appalled. Gideon was crying. Tears escaped from the bandage hiding the ruined socket, and ran down his cheek.

"You were touched to come back here, Gideon," he said gruffly. "Even the Seneca ain't as stubborn as you. They made their treaties and moved on." He spat derisively. "Now stop that. It's embarrassing, boy. You're as sentimental as a woman."

Polly was back, with Samuel in her arms. She sank to her knees beside Gideon and laid the baby in his lap. When she saw the state he was in, she forgot to scold, and pulled him to her, resting his head against her heart.

"I was wrong to say those things, Polly. It was fool's talk, and I'm sorry." He looked up at her. "It's just that a woman's sense of honor ain't the same as a man's."

"You're such a simpleton," she said, stroking his back. "That's complete and utter nonsense, Gideon. It's exactly the same. But you have children, so you must stay alive. Sometimes honor can just go to blazes."

"I've ruined us."

"No, you haven't. You've had bad luck. You think with your heart, Gideon. I wouldn't love you so much if you didn't."

"I'm so tired, Pol."

She studied Gideon's face as he lifted the baby on his arm and nuzzled him.

"Thank God you think with your head, darlin'," he whispered, handing the child to her. "Mine hasn't stopped spinning yet. If you want us to leave . . . for Jenuchshadego or Canada, or whatever, we'll go. I won't decide for us anymore. I can't."

"You needn't decide anything today, dear," she said gently. "We have to wait for Livy and Ephraim to come back anyway."

She watched John help Gideon to his feet. Gideon was dizzy and had to sit back for a moment. When he was finally standing, then walking, he held his head slightly to the left .

"John?" she whispered, following along, watching Gideon's cautious steps. "When you go to the village, go to Tyler's store. You can promise him all my butter next season if you have to, but bring home another gun. Mrs. Clairemont would get the vapors, but as long as those vermin are in the neighborhood, I'm carrying my own."

Chapter 24

They rushed headlong through the forest. Rising Hawk set a furious pace, leaving Livy floundering along behind. She didn't dare stop to form a decent bundle of their blankets, but carried them overflowing her arms, picking up burrs and dried leaves as she ran.

"Shouldn't we get off, Rising Hawk? Shouldn't we hide?"

Rising Hawk made an abrupt motion with his arm to quiet her. She was yelling loud enough for three girls. And it was presumptuous of her to offer advice. She was ignorant. A Seneca girl would have kept her mouth shut and her eyes open.

"We can't really outrun them, can we? Not in their own country?"

He stopped and grabbed her roughly by the back of the neck, drawing her to him. "They will not catch us if you will be quiet and move!" he whispered harshly. He was shaking, whether with anger or fear, Livy couldn't tell. But he didn't look fearless. Not at all like the warriors of her uncle's stories.

He didn't want to tell her about the dogs. If their pursuers used dogs, he and Livy would have to take to the streams to kill the scent. But unless they laid a false trail to mislead them, the trackers would simply follow the stream east, out of Seneca territory. He would have to change direction. Take them deeper into it. No one would expect that. But then what? North to Canada? Or should they take their chances with the Shawnee? Since their victory over the American army two winters ago on the Wabash, the Shawnee had been contemptuous of any Seneca who hadn't joined them.

Suddenly aware he was holding her too tightly, he released her. "Just be quiet, Livy. We'll be all right. Just try to stay quiet." He was relieved to see she didn't really understand the danger. And he was grateful there wasn't time to explain. Delay could be fatal. Their only sure chance lay in staying ahead of their pursuers.

Livy couldn't keep up. She had stamina, but no speed. She fell farther and farther behind. Rising Hawk finally stopped to rest, opened his bearskin pouch, and half filled the depression of her hand with parched corn. "You have it," she whispered. "I'm too tired."

"Don't be stubborn. Eat."

Livy shook her head.

There was no time. He pinched her nose. When she opened to breathe, he forced the corn in. His sudden violence frightened her. She gave in, but he stood over her anyway, until she swallowed it all.

The only water was some brackish stuff caught in the rotted trunk of a tree. When she revolted, he threatened to push her face into it and make her lap it like a dog.

"You are fortunate," he said, as she glared at him reproachfully. "Sometimes there is nothing to drink but your own urine."

Livy scooped up the stale water. "I think I'd prefer that," she whispered, forcing it down.

If they were going to be taken, it would be soon. Rising Hawk moved them off the trail and through a difficult tangle of brush in an effort to confuse their pursuers. It was futile if they were using dogs, but if they weren't, it would buy him and Livy time. Blackberry bushes made up some of the thicket, and Livy scratched her arm from wrist to elbow. Noiselessly she folded onto the ground, clutching her arm and rocking against the pain. Rising Hawk crouched beside her without reprimand and let her alone. He had no idea what he would do if they were captured. He had taken Livy away, hoping the village would be content just to be rid of her. But if Sassafras died, the sachems would have to hold an inquiry. After that . . . he couldn't stand to think of it. Witches were executed every year.

Livy sat with her back to him, tallying up his faults. Her arm was bleeding, and it was growing cold—the kind of cold that soaked into her like water and made her shake. Rising Hawk had finally bundled and tied the blankets. When she asked for one, he shook his head and put a finger to his lips. She gave him another black mark.

They traveled the rest of the night in silence, every nerve alert for the sight or sound of human beings. Rising Hawk knew the way by feel, and Livy was beginning to believe in his ability to navigate the forest and get them home safely. For the first time since they'd left the village, she could breathe without being aware of it. Rising Hawk stopped suddenly, knelt, and stripped wintergreen leaves from their waxy stems. He handed some to Livy. "Chew them," he whispered. "The bears will smell our approach and keep away." They were a puny weapon, but having no other defense, she took the leaves. She was suddenly aware of her breathing again.

Livy and Rising Hawk had been gone for about an hour when Pretty Girl came through the door, her face alight with excitement. "It was a baby," she said breathlessly. "A very tiny baby, hardly bigger than a minnow. I saw it. She bled, and that was what caused it. She still bleeds," she added, "but her grandmother has made tea to slow the pains and thinks it will stop soon."

Shadow and Dream Teller exchanged glances. A very small baby. It wasn't Rising Hawk then. He had been gone five moons, at least. "What has been decided?" Shadow asked.

"She did not lose it deliberately. She didn't even know she had it." Pretty Girl blushed. She was uncomfortable discussing women's secrets with a young man.

"But the witch?" her mother said. "What have they decided about the witch?"

"They think it more likely a menstruating girl may have been careless and drunk from a gourd just before Sassafras did, causing her to lose the baby. They aren't thinking about witches now. They aren't concerned about my brother or Livy at all, either. Now they are just curious as to who the lover is, but Sassafras is asleep and likely to be asleep for a long time, her grandmother says."

"Should we go after them?" Cold Keeper asked. "Or would that frighten them unduly?" He laughed. "We don't want to arouse that girl."

"Let them go," Buffalo Creek Woman said. Her wrist was soaking in cold water from the river. It was nothing more, after all, than a bruise. "Let Gideon deal with them. That quiet girl turned out to be nothing but trouble. I suppose it's not her fault, but if she comes visiting again, I will have to make sure she is tamed first." She smiled slightly. It pleased her to see that the girl had an independent spirit after all. Meanwhile, the wheel was here, and she had had more than enough practice to be able to finish filling the bobbins with thread. It would do for now. Next spring she would talk Gideon into building her a loom.

Chapter 25

Rising Hawk slowed their pace the next day. He was worried about Livy. She had taken a hard blow to the ribs. There was no telling how serious. She wouldn't let him see. But the bruises on her face had darkened, and he was afraid she was ill. Even though she had made no complaints since he'd forced her to drink, he knew he had pushed her as far as he dared.

By midday he had dropped companionably to her side and, out of concern for her injuries, taken the blanket bundle off her hands. He smiled now, and occasionally stopped to show her an interesting track or point out a view. By the time evening rolled around, he was his old self again.

"They are not following us," he admitted finally. "Perhaps Shadow and Dream Teller set them on the wrong trail after all."

"How do you know for sure?"

"Because they would have caught us by now, if that was their intent," he said. "This morning, while you slept, I climbed some trees to look. I ran back a great distance. There are no signs at all that anyone is following." He smiled warmly and patted the top of her head. "Stop worrying. They have let us go. They could have caught us the first night, if they had wanted to."

They were too weary to hunt even the smallest game. Squirrels chattered overhead as Livy stripped some half-ripe grapes from their vines, then sat quietly wrapped in a blanket. Rising Hawk pulled cattail roots from a pond and offered her the last of the parched corn, but she had no appetite. Without comment, he watched her take a few listless bites, then put the food aside. While he ate, she looked up through dark and tangled trees at the stars.

Rising Hawk pointed out a cloudy mass to the north. "Someday I will tell you the story of the Seven Brothers."

"Why not now?"

"The *djoge o* forbid it. The birds have not yet flown south, and the bears are still putting on fur and fat."

"What's that?"

"The *djoge o* are little spirits, like those tiny creatures in the stories Polly tells my niece and nephew. Fairies? They keep watch, because if a storyteller tells these stories too soon, the animals and birds may stop to listen and forget to do what they must to survive the winter."

"What happens if you break that rule?"

"They send a reminder. A bee might sting your lip; whatever they choose, it hurts."

"You broke that rule last spring when you told us about the turtle warrior."

"Yes. I'm wiser now."

"Were you punished?"

"I put up with you and your rudeness for a whole summer season. Some might call that a punishment." She made no reply. For a while, the only sound was him gnawing on a cattail root.

"Are you a real storyteller?" she asked finally.

He swallowed the last of his share and held out a piece for her. If she didn't eat something, he would be carrying her tomorrow. "If you mean, would anyone else think of me as one, no. I want to be, but I don't know enough yet. That's why I always spend my winters at Jenuchshadego. After the hunt, the storyteller tells stories every night."

She took the root. "So you'll be going back this winter?"

"No, sooner. As soon as I get you home to Gideon. I would rather not be caught in an early snowstorm."

For the first time Livy realized Rising Hawk would be going away. Not forever, of course, but for now. They weren't exactly kindred spirits, but she couldn't imagine life without him.

Rising Hawk bent to kindle the fire. After a few moments with the flint and steel, the charred linen took hold. He fed little pieces of rotten wood into it, followed by some bone-dry twigs. Then he sat back. It was obvious in the firelight that there were tears dropping off Livy's chin. She wouldn't eat, and now she was crying. He moved to her side and laid his hand on her forehead. Fever. Not much of one, but a complication. "Your face is hot," he said quietly.

Livy wiped her sleeve across her face. It was an unattractive gesture. Rising Hawk never found crying women appealing. Most of them looked awful, and Livy was no exception. "I'm not hot," she whispered. "Cold." She drew a sniffling breath.

"Fever," he said, and put a comforting arm around her. "Don't cry," he said. "I have seen you much sicker than this. You did not cry then."

"When I had settler's fever? I didn't cry, but you almost did."

"Two days ago, you were in your first battle. You were wounded. You bled. You didn't cry then."

Livy let out a snort, then gasped. "Don't make me laugh, Rising Hawk. It hurts." He leaned against a tree trunk and let her arrange herself against him. She pulled the blanket to her chin.

"When Father Clairemont was teaching me English, he was fond of saying, 'There is a first time for everything.' For example, you hit my cousin very hard on the head with that firewood. That was the first time you tried to kill, wasn't it?"

"I wasn't trying to kill him, Rising Hawk. Stop it."

"You do not know that my uncle proposed a new name for you. Two names really. We should choose between them. Do you prefer Throws Her Firewood or Mankiller? Is it possible that in that place you come from, they were afraid of you and happy to see you go?"

"You have to stop now," she said in a strained voice. "I don't think they're broken, but a couple of my ribs hurt, and you're making it worse."

He touched her side gently. "Does this hurt?" he asked, his voice full of concern.

"I guess not. No more than a bruise hurts." She looked up. His face was five inches away, and he wasn't looking at her side. He was looking straight into her eyes.

"You are a most unusual girl," he whispered. "What will you be like in two or three winters?"

She kissed him without hesitation, so it was natural that he should embrace her. He was surprised and a little confused and held her gingerly, afraid to hurt her. Her response was to kiss him again. His caresses got bolder, and she suddenly found herself pressed hard against his neck, inhaling his smoky scent. His breath tickled her ear, and his lips touched her gently as he whispered something. She couldn't understand his words, but they were pleasant and soft and sent a thrill down her back.

When she didn't protest, he began to touch her. First her ears, then her neck. His lips brushed her closed eyes. Livy held on, puzzled and drowning in sensation. She had always been taught that men were just burdens to be borne. This was something neither her aunt nor Polly had ever even hinted at.

Rising Hawk moved slightly, his hand sliding very slowly down her neck. Gently he traced the outline of her breasts, then slipped his hand under the fabric. At this her eyes flew open.

"Don't," she said.

"You don't like it?" he asked.

She pulled back. "Just don't."

"Why not?" He had moved his hand, but now it ran, distractingly, up and down the inside of her arm.

"Only married folks do that, otherwise it's fornication and a sin." She sounded indignant.

He tried to keep the amusement out of his voice when he said, "I have read some of the Bible. This is not fornication." His hand was at the nape of her neck now. She shivered.

"Maybe not quite, but it's close."

"Perhaps, but I can be quite delightful without fornication." He nuzzled her neck, breathing very lightly into her ear. "Let me show you."

She closed her eyes for a moment. She was pretty sure it was wrong, but what he was doing was so nice. How had she gotten herself into such an awkward position?

"Let me show you. It's all right. Sh . . . sh." He lifted the braid off the back of her neck and blew very gently. "Good, huh? Here." He brushed the same spot with his lips.

"Rising Hawk . . . Oh, that is nice."

"I can tell stories with my fingers, too. Did you know that?"

He could, and she had completely lost the thread of the argument, when his hand strayed into her dress front again. This time she pushed him away.

"Stop it, Rising Hawk. No. No more stories. I mean it. I need to survive, too . . . same as those birds and the bears that your *djoge o* protect from storytellers."

Rising Hawk leaned back lazily. His eyes looked sleepy, and he smiled at her in a way that reminded her of a cat. "Livy, perhaps we made a mistake. Not now. I mean back in the village. We thought there was nothing serious with us, but . . . Look, bears are solitary creatures."

"So am I," Livy said hastily.

"You are not as solitary as you think," he said. "No human being can survive all alone."

"I can if I have to. If you won't stay and be my friend, I can."

"Livy, what do you want? Should I be your father?" He laughed. "Perhaps that is the solution. You should come back with me. Then you can persuade my mother to adopt you. You would be my sister, Livy, and safe."

She looked at him carefully. He realized with a sinking feeling that she didn't know if he was serious or not. How very young she really was. Fifteen! It was almost indecent. He frowned.

"Don't be so angry, Rising Hawk! I'm never getting married. You know that. I just want us to go on being friends. I never should have kissed you. Besides, you're an Indian. I can't marry an Indian."

Rising Hawk sat up. "What?"

"Look, I'm sorry, Rising Hawk, but you're the one who said no one should ever marry someone their family thinks would be bad for them. My uncle would have killed us."

"Your uncle is dead. Gideon's your family now. He won't kill either of us."

"Your grandmother wouldn't like it any more than my uncle. I don't fit in, Rising Hawk. They think I'm odd." She looked down at her lap. "And maybe I am, but I just . . . can't . . . breathe there. Can you understand that? There are too many people, watching all the time. At least in a white village we don't have to share a house with the neighbors. Besides, what are we arguing about? I've realized over the past few days that you are my best friend in the world, and nothing will change that."

Rising Hawk spoke very quietly. "We're arguing because I want to make love to you, and I probably shouldn't."

"It was my fault, Rising Hawk. I'm sorry. I started it. I didn't realize—"

"Livy, stop. You never used to talk at all, and now you talk too much. Listen to me for a moment. There is a medicine ceremony where you must dip water from the water road . . . the river, you understand? When you dip into the current, you must not dip against it, or the water spirits are disturbed and the medicine will not work. But this is just what you do. You always dip against the current. The medicine works when you accept what life gives you."

"I'm never getting married. To you or anyone. It's not safe."

Rising Hawk smiled gently and leaned forward, taking hold of the medallion he had given her. "Livy, you are very young and very, very stubborn. But someday, in two, maybe three, years, you will lose this fear you have and you will marry a man, and we will both be very disappointed if that man is not me." He pulled a little on the necklace, making her lean toward him. "Life is so simple, Livy. We will take care of each other, that's all."

Livy sat very still. "It's not that simple," she said quietly. "If they had caught us, would you have gone against them? Your uncle and father and everyone?"

He stared at her. After what seemed an eternity, he averted his eyes and very slowly released the necklace.

Chapter 26

Lawson had just about given up on the fools in this town. Knox had been fired three days ago for that little incident at the renegade's place. Fired and replaced by some fancy engineering student from Canandaigua. The boy couldn't be above twenty-two years old. Plain made him sick.

What was worse, that mayor, the sorriest excuse for a white man he ever saw, had been talking with the company. Now they were supposed to make restitution for Gunn's place by giving over half the timber they'd set aside that summer, so the heathen could rebuild. Restitution to a traitor! They were expected to do the hauling, too.

Lawson grumbled and complained until he'd chewed it over and decided that maybe he'd had a little restitution of his own. All the while they'd been gruntin' and sweatin' the loads in, Gunn had watched them, leaning against a tree with a rifle in his hand, a bandage over his eye socket, looking sickly. There was satisfaction in knowing that at least they'd put the fear of God into them snakes. Even Gunn's pretty woman carried a rifle now.

Anyway, he wasn't going to be making restitution to a renegade for much longer. Soon as he had himself a deer and dried some venison, he was collecting his wages and clearing out. He was heading east. Gonna move into a nice, safe town and marry a widow or something. Never have to lay eyes on an Indian again.

Livy's fever hadn't gone away, so the next morning Rising Hawk made her stay in bed until noon. Neither of them spoke much. They both seemed to feel that there was nothing more to say, though Rising Hawk kept running last night's conversation in his head, and Livy, when he didn't know it, watched his every move as if trying to commit him to memory.

By late afternoon they were back on the trail, and Rising Hawk broke the truce, speaking as if he were simply picking up from where they'd left off. "Anyone living faces death any moment. Women have babies every day."

"And some of them die."

"But most of them don't. Have some courage."

"Have you noticed, you're always accusing me of being a coward?"

"I'm sorry."

"No, you're not. But I'm not a coward, Rising Hawk. I'm using every bit of courage I have right now to tell you no . . . even though I'm sick and tired and my head aches."

"I'm sorry."

"You know what I think? I think it's easier for a woman to just go along and stay quiet and give up. My Aunt Mary used to do it. Polly does that with Gideon all the time. I won't do it. I'm just as stubborn as you are."

"More."

She smiled and said, "Look, we don't need to change anything. Can't we just be like before? You don't really have to go right back to Jenuchshadego."

"You mean, you want to go on being my little brother? Livy, you don't appreciate the fact that I am a man."

"And you don't seem to appreciate that I'm not quite a woman."

Livy had stopped caring that her uncle would have hated Rising Hawk. In the cold theology he'd taught her, it was God's law that like pair with like. Hadn't Noah paired the animals with their own kind? Now that she was older and understood such things better, she wanted to ask her uncle why it had never occurred to him that if God was really set against the pairing of different-colored people, He would have made it a mechanical impossibility. Uncle John would have whipped her for it, but she would have asked him anyway.

Rising Hawk's arguments hadn't changed her mind. But the thought of him going away was almost more than she could bear. And the more she studied him, the way he walked and listened, even the way he laughed at her, the more frantic she became. Finally, when they were within running distance of Gideon's home, desperation got the better of her pride.

"I've given it a lot of thought, Rising Hawk, and I've decided something."

"About us?"

"Yes. No, wait; don't turn around. There's something I want you to know, but it's shocking, and I don't know if I can say the words aloud if you're looking at me."

"Then I won't look at you, and I give you my word," he said, laying a hand to his heart and smiling, "I will not be shocked by anything you say to me."

Livy took a deep breath and hugged her blanket bundle tighter. "Here's what I've been thinking: In the Bible the kings sometimes had lots of wives. More than two anyway. Two's nothing, compared to what those kings had." She hesitated. "I guess I could stand it if you had Sassafras for one kind of wife, and me for another."

Rising Hawk stood still while the meaning of her words sank in. "You would do that? Rather than be parted?"

"Don't you see, Rising Hawk? You could have a real wife—for babies and such—and a companion wife all at the same time."

"Sometimes a Seneca man will have two wives, Livy, but it is unusual, and not considered proper. The better families do not practice this. And *your* idea—this I have never heard of."

"Well, you know, I really wouldn't mind, Rising Hawk. This way we could be together, forever. Sassafras isn't so bad, and even if we decide to live with Gideon and Polly, the two of us could do the farming and you could hunt. It would be almost like Jenuchshadego."

"And you think Polly would approve of this? Father Clairemont wouldn't. He would be very shocked, and Polly thinks a great deal of Father Clairemont."

"Well, we don't have to tell Father Clairemont, do we?"

"I'm sorry," he said, turning slowly and trying hard not to grin. "I'm sorry. I know I promised but . . . " He started laughing. He was laughing so hard that he didn't hear the crack of a twig on the trail ahead of him.

Gideon had heard from Mr. Wilkes about Ephraim. His new master was eager to part with him, but not until they had finished the corn harvest. It seemed Eph had put them a little behind.

Meanwhile, John and Gideon were hunting up the last of the deer. If they could take just one, they could leave Polly and the children for the ten days it would take them to run over to Jenuchshadego and back. They could fetch Rising Hawk and Livy and probably convince his mother to let Runs Faster come visit. Together they could transport enough corn for half the winter anyway. Gideon was trying to calculate just how many packs they could manage when he heard the shot. It was far to the south of him, while John had gone north. He probably wouldn't have bothered investigating, but he heard the faint echo of a woman's scream.

Lawson saw the savage before the savage saw him. He was a young fellow. He had a gun, but he seemed to be distracted by something behind him on the trail. As a matter of fact, he was laughing when Lawson pulled the trigger.

Rising Hawk stumbled before Livy heard the shot. He had been laughing at her, while her face grew hot with shame, then he'd sat down on the trail, and only then had she heard the report. The man with the gun was just ahead of them on the trail, kneeling and partially hidden behind an oak. She screamed, and he locked eyes with her.

What in the world? Lawson didn't know what to make of the white girl who had come up behind the savage. She wasn't dressed like a Seneca, though she was toting a pack like one of their women and wearing moccasins. But something was wrong. Her face was bruised. Why, that dirty son of a bitch! Lawson hadn't even meant to shoot, but the hand of Providence had guided him. He'd rescued the girl. She was still screaming, but she had the sense to pick up the bastard's rifle. Now why was she pointing it at him? Poor thing must have been driven out of her head by her ordeal.

"Lay that rifle down!" she screamed. The words rolled out of her in a powerful wave. Lawson set the gun on the ground and put his hands up where she could see them.

"Look, now, little missy, I put it down. You'd best move that gun away from me. I don't want it going off accidental." She had stopped not ten feet away, too close to miss, and her hands were shaking.

"Tend to him," she said coolly, her voice unnaturally loud in the hushed woods. "Tend to him now, or I'll kill you." She kept her distance. She might be scared, but she wasn't stupid. Lawson had to give her credit.

The Indian was sitting up, yanking at the leggings on his right leg. Blood was pouring out, obscuring the wound. When Lawson approached, the boy drew his knife and scooted backward on his good leg. His hand was slippery with blood, and he was going green around the mouth.

"Rising Hawk." The girl was gentle, but her voice held authority. "It was an accident. He didn't mean to shoot; did you, sir?"

Lawson shook his head. "Naw. It was a mistake. I guess I figured you for a deer." It wasn't a complete lie. Even now he wasn't sure if he'd shot him deliberately or not.

"Please put the knife down. He won't hurt you."

The boy looked at her a long moment, then laid it down. He was sweating now, and spat, without taking his eyes off Lawson.

"Don't worry. If he tries anything, I'll shoot him in the head, just like one of your gourd targets. Only this time it won't be an arrow made to bring down chickadees." She narrowed her eyes at Lawson. He noticed her hands had stopped shaking.

He kept his mouth shut, took hold of the boy's shoulders, and laid him down. Then he picked up the knife and, keeping his movements slow and deliberate, began to cut away the soggy cloth.

Chapter 27

It was a lucky shot, going clear through his calf and missing the bone. He wouldn't even lose his foot. Too bad. It looked terrible, though, and since Lawson hadn't actually tried to stanch the blood flow, the fellow was as weak as a blade of grass and nearly as green.

The girl was growing impatient. She ventured close enough to poke him in the back. Lawson didn't appreciate no pip-squeak girl pointing a gun at him.

"I'm sorry, sis," he said, pulling off his hat, "but he's about done for." He settled back on his haunches to assess the situation. The girl's gray eyes were as wide as Spanish dollars as she scurried over to look, all panicked and shaking.

"But you haven't even tied it. He's still bleeding."

She raised the gun level to Lawson's eyes. "Fix it."

He smiled and shook his head. She'd let herself get too close. It was a simple matter to grab the gun.

He boxed her ears some for being so eager to shoot him. Then stood aside to let her tend to the animal. She tore some strips from the hem of her shift and tied up the wound. The savage's eyes were fluttering open and closed. She kept talking to him in English. Ordering him, sharp, to wake up.

Lawson watched dumbly for a while. She was skillful, and there was something about the tender way she handled the varmint that aroused his suspicions.

"What are you doing out here? This filthy animal steal you from someone?"

The girl ignored him. Her silence was a dismissal. He wasn't worth talking to. Lawson's fingers itched to slap her again.

"I asked you a question, missy. Answer me." This time he caught her by the wrist. She looked up at him, indignant.

"Let go. He needs water. We'll have to find some."

Lawson caught her other wrist and pulled her across the boy's body. "You ain't answered me yet. How'd you come to be with him? Where's your ma? Your folks?"

The girl cried out at his rough handling. She was hurt somewhere. She pulled weakly in an attempt to free herself.

"I don't have any. He's my master's brother. He's looking after me. We're friends." She pulled again. "Please let go."

The savage reacted to her voice. He opened his eyes at Lawson and said, clearly, "Don't hurt her. Leave us now. We have nothing you could want."

Lawson dropped the girl. She had to belong to Gunn, like that boy they'd gotten away from him. He'd been bound out to some other farmer and left Gunn seriously shorthanded. Lawson smiled. Now he had the girl as well. Nothing illegal about it, either.

Wilkes had called Gunn a "corrupting influence." Only a heathen household would allow a girl that age to traipse around the woods with this animal. He'd take the girl into town. Turn her over to Wilkes to pray over. Get her a new place, too. It irked him, some, that this scum took him for a thief. Well, it was a terrible shame, but it looked like he'd have to leave this fellow for the wolves.

The girl fussed and hollered when he hauled her off the boy again to tie her wrists. He was surprised at the words the little priss knew. He left a good long lead to drag her by. When he bent over the savage to pick up the rifle, the girl made a dive at the boy. Lawson had to pull her up short and he hurt her again. The boy looked heartbroke when she cried out, but could only fix Lawson with a murderous look.

"I got her now, and there ain't a damn thing you can do about it, is there?" It was puzzling to see the look on the boy's face. Lawson had never seen an Indian with feelings before.

Gideon and John came upon Rising Hawk not long after. They could see that there had been a struggle. Someone, probably Livy, had been dragged over the ground. There were more drag marks at the edge of the clearing. Her heels had dug in. At that rate she'd be losing her moccasins before long. She was leaving a good trail, but they had to get Rising Hawk safe first. Livy would have to shift for herself.

Despite the pain her side was causing her, Livy kept fighting. She was desperate to get back to Rising Hawk. In his weakened condition, anything might happen. She tried screaming, but Lawson smacked her bruised cheek. She kept up the heel dragging, until Lawson slammed her up against a tree and pinned her by the throat.

"You'll walk and you'll walk smart, or I'll hurt you—and it won't be no little smack 'cross your mouth, neither."

Her eyes were big and frightened then. It was pleasurable, and he smirked and relaxed his hold a little. His teeth were blotchy brown and yellow and green, like river rocks. She turned her face a little. It was a slight movement, but it showed her revulsion.

"Well, you're a fine young lady. Too good for me, ain't you? Just real special. You're mighty concerned about that savage. Why is that, Duchess? Could it be that you bed with that critter?"

Livy gasped. She shook her head as much as his encircling fingers would allow. He saw the blush spreading over her face.

"That's why you're making such a fuss. You've been giving yourself to that filthy animal, and you ain't even captive or nothing." He spat in disgust. Then his face changed, and he leaned lazily against her, enveloping them both in his vile scent.

"Tell me, Duchess, since you're laying with one, is it true what they say about them Seneca bucks? Can they really . . . ?" Leering, he put his mouth to her ear and whispered the rest.

She turned pale at his repulsive words and was struggling to get free, when he suddenly pressed his whiskery mouth to hers, closed all around her lips, and pushed his tongue against her clenched teeth. He held her there long enough to make her good and mad, then let her loose. She let out a yell, spit over and over as if she'd swallowed a bug, and wiped at her mouth with her bound wrists.

He laughed out loud as he caught at the rope and yanked her forward. She was a baby. Didn't know nothing. That was obvious. Whatever was between her and that fella hadn't gone very far. He'd heard them Seneca were awful prudish. It was the only good he knew of them.

Lawson had no more trouble with the girl after the kiss. It had scared her more than a beating and kept her scared even after they got out of the forest cover and onto the new road.

The prospect of causing Gunn more trouble put Lawson in a rare holiday mood. He talked to the girl to settle her down, regardless that she seemed disinclined to talk to him.

"You New England folk weren't here for the war, but I was. My whole family was butchered at Cherry Valley. The things I seen. . . . I was only a little fellow, younger than you." Lawson paused and drew a deep breath. He had never told the story stone sober before. "For some reason I was spared. The raiders knocked me on the head and left. When I came to, they'd already scalped the others, right down to my year-old baby brother."

Livy glanced up at him. His lip trembled.

"Turned out my little sister Mandy was still alive, too. She was scalped and a bloody mess, but she was conscious and knew me. I lifted her onto our hove-in front door and dragged her outside into the snow."

Lawson was gratified to see that the little chit by his side was in tears and dabbing at her eyes.

"I ran for my sled so I could move us someplace safe just as they came back. There was nothin' I could do. I ducked into the woodshed and saw a Tory pig bring a tomahawk down on Mandy. She was six years old. I still hear that thud in my dreams."

Livy wiped at her eyes. "That's terrible," she whispered, and hiccuped.

"Sit down, sis. It's all right now; here." Livy sat, and Lawson untied her wrists. "There now, you walk along regular, and I won't use no more rope."

"Mister, I understand why you hate Indians and Tories so."

"Well now, you're a fair-minded duchess. Just been led astray, I reckon."

"But Rising Hawk was only a baby when those terrible things happened. You can't blame him."

"A Indian's a Indian, sis. I seen firsthand what they're capable of. Don't try and fool yourself. It comes natural to them. That fella's done plenty of evil."

"No, he hasn't. He's probably the kindest human being I've ever known, excepting Polly Gunn."

Lawson's face softened a little at the mention of Polly. Nonetheless, he took her arm in silence and made her walk on.

"Please, please let me go. Even if he isn't bleeding now, he's sick and weak, and what happens if a bear or a panther finds him there?"

"Then that'll be one less savage to worry about."

"Let me go! You have no rights over me. You're probably breaking the law. You broke the law shooting Rising Hawk. That was no accident, was it? You shot him on purpose."

She twisted suddenly and bit the filthy hand holding her. She ran and was off the road and deep into a pine grove before he caught up and knocked her to the ground. He had his foot on her back before she knew she was down.

"I oughta knock your teeth out for that. I will, if you try that again, you little hellcat. And don't talk to me about no damn law. I know all about rights. Here's rights for you. I'm bigger than you, I run faster than you, and I got a gun. Them's my rights."

Despite her pain and fatigue, Livy struggled furiously to get up. But he held her down until the rage passed out of her and she lay still. Then he let her up and tied her hands again, preaching all the while.

"What you do not understand, child, is that a white woman who lives with savages of her own volition is lower than one of them Indian girls. And a white woman who breeds with them is lower than a whore even. You are a nice little girl and too young to know the damage you are doing. I am saving you from yourself."

Chapter 28

Eph was curled up on the straw tick by the fireplace. He ran upstairs to get Mr. Wilkes to unbar the door when Lawson's heavy hand began to pound on it.

Mrs. Wilkes came grumbling after her husband, clutching a wrap to her throat, wondering who could be calling at half past ten and ordering Eph back to bed in the same breath. When Eph saw it was Livy, he was up again and all over her with delighted cries, until Mrs. Wilkes saw his embraces were hurting her.

"Sit here, child," she ordered, indicating a bench at the table. "Ephraim Pelton, leave her alone a moment. Sit with her if you must, but don't squeeze so. Livy, what in heaven's name are you doing out at this hour with this . . . gentleman? And where did you get that black eye? If I didn't know you, child, I'd think you'd been fist fighting."

Livy did look a sight. Her eye had swollen a little and turned deep purple. The bruises on her face were dark. Her outer dress was stiff with blood. Ragged bits of shift dangled from the back, and her stockings had fallen down and seeped into her scuffed-up moccasins.

Lawson offered his explanation, that he'd found her alone in the forest with a Seneca warrior, supposed to be Gunn's brother. Eph, wondering where Rising Hawk was, confirmed that Livy had gone to Jenuchshadego. It was the first time he had mentioned it to anyone. He was rather proud of that. Since his fatal slip to the road crew had gotten Gideon in such trouble, he'd been guarding his tongue carefully.

Livy looked ill and miserable. She started to explain, but after a few moments Mr. Wilkes exploded in anger, abusing Gideon for his lack of sense. Then he wondered at Polly for living with such a crackbrain. As an afterthought, he offered Lawson a chair and a brandy. Mrs. Wilkes had already uncorked the bottle and was encouraging Livy to swallow some.

"You poor child," Mr. Wilkes said, looking flummoxed. "I blame myself, of course. What was it you were supposed to do? Spin? It seems Gunn now considers himself a missionary, or perhaps a government agent? It is quite clear you must be removed from the influence of those misguided people at once." His eyes lit on Ephraim, who was holding Livy's hand and looking lost. He was due to be delivered back to Gunn in the morning.

"If there was an alternative, young fellow, I would not return you, either. Unfortunately, you have made your bed and must lie in it. Unless a tinker should turn up at our door in need of an apprentice by tomorrow morning, you must go back. The Gunthers have been quite vocal in appraising your work. No one else will have you."

Eph teared up and began to sniffle. He and Livy were going to be separated once and for all. It was all his fault.

"I cannot understand how a man with children of his own, and one of them a daughter, too, could allow this child, virtually unprotected, to go into the last stronghold of wild Seneca in the state. And to live among them? People with no understanding of or sympathy for Christian values? It is a disgrace!"

After this speech, Livy took a cautious sip of Mrs. Wilkes's brandy. She could trace its descent all the way to her stomach. Her nose burned on the inside. She took another sip. It was going quickly to her head, her stomach being empty, finally, of parched corn.

Lawson was getting into the spirit of the occasion. "It was Providence directed my hand so I was able to take care of that savage I found her with."

"Good man," Wilkes said, giving his shoulder a hearty shake. He stopped abruptly. "What, precisely, do you mean by 'take care of'?"

"Shot him."

"Shot him?" Wilkes said. "Do you mean dead?" Livy laid her head on her arms.

"No, no," Lawson corrected him. "It was a clean shot through the leg. He's alive, unless a panther got to him."

Now Ephraim began to cry in earnest.

"Well, where is he, then?" Wilkes asked, moving toward the door. "Have you left him in the yard?"

"No. Not exactly," Lawson said.

Wilkes looked puzzled. "You don't mean to tell me you left him out in the woods somewhere?"

Lawson nodded. "I couldn't very well drag him. He warn't in a fit condition to walk. I had trouble enough bringing the girl."

"Good Lord, man." Wilkes wiped at his brow. "Was it self-defense?"

Lawson nodded again. "Yes, sir, it was. He had a gun."

"Did he threaten you with it?"

Lawson glanced sideways at Livy. "Yes, he did."

Livy raised her head from the table. "He did not. That man is a liar."

"Deliverance," Mr. Wilkes said firmly. "Did the Indian threaten Mr. Lawson, or didn't he?"

"He did not. And he's not 'the Indian.' His name is Rising Hawk, and we were talking about getting married, after a fashion, and Rising Hawk had his back turned when this man shot him from behind a tree." Her voice shook, and she fought back tears.

Mrs. Wilkes turned deadly pale. "Married?" she gasped.

Mr. Wilkes grasped his hands behind his back. "Mr. Lawson, this is a serious situation. Tomorrow morning, at first light, we fetch the Indian."

"Why?"

"The Indian agent at Canandaigua will want to talk to him. Provided he can talk."

"What for?"

"Because, young man, this is a treaty matter. You can't just go around, willy-nilly, shooting Indians."

"I didn't sign no treaty," Lawson said, cradling his gun.

"Mr. Lawson, we are not at war."

Lawson surveyed the room. "I got plans, and they don't include dealing with the law. I won't stand for no interference from you over some damned Indian. I brought the girl, and that's enough. Now, you tell your old woman to bring me some provisions and a blanket, and I'll be on my way." His hand caressed the handle of the long knife strapped to his thigh. "You know you ain't enough to stop me, old man. If you try it, by the time I get through with you, the village is gonna think some renegade Shawnee spent the night. I won't leave no witnesses."

"Come with me. No, my dear." Mr. Wilkes put out a hand to stop his wife as she rose, looking frightened. "I will deal with him."

"You two," Lawson said, indicating Mrs. Wilkes and Ephraim. "Down cellar." Ephraim took Livy's hand. "No, boy," Lawson said, brandishing the long, gouging nails of his right hand. "Just you and the old woman." Eph winced at the sight of those claws, but held on defiantly until Livy gave him a gentle push. Lawson locked them in.

"Livy," Mr. Wilkes said, with an uneasy glance at Lawson. "Run upstairs, child, and get me a blanket."

When Livy returned, the men were at the back door. Lawson had a packet of food slung from his shoulder. As she handed him the blanket, he caught her wrist and pulled her toward the door.

"What the devil are you doing?" Wilkes shouted.

"She's for sale, ain't she?"

"Not under these circumstances, Mr. Lawson. You aren't a homesteader. And if you don't turn yourself in, you're a fugitive."

"Look, Wilkes, I won't force myself on the girl. But she needs educating. You folks ain't done right by her."

"She'll be looked after."

"You bound her out to a Tory spy, Wilkes. She's been living in a Seneca town, and her bosom companion is a Seneca warrior. I don't call that looking after her."

He tugged on Livy, and she resisted.

"Now look, sis. I'll take care of you, like you was one of my poor, dead sisters."

Livy shook her head.

"There now, Lawson," Wilkes said, blocking the door. "Let her go."

"Your Seneca friend ain't got the chance of a banked catfish. He's as good as dead."

"If he is, then you're his murderer."

"Yeah," Lawson said, with a smile.

"And I'll kill you for it. I swear I will. The first chance I get."

The smile faded as Lawson turned cold eyes on her. "I believe you are serious, sis, and if you're that far gone, it'd be a kindness to kill you now."

Mr. Wilkes stepped between them. "Young man, she's only a child. I don't believe you're a coward, and only a coward would do such a thing."

Lawson stared dumbly at the old man for a moment, then shook his head. "She ain't worth it, Wilkes. I'll leave her to you. I ain't hanging for that thing, nor the Indian, neither."

They didn't even hear his footsteps as he disappeared into the night.

Mrs. Wilkes was considerably shaken. She sat down heavily and took a sip of brandy, directly from the bottle. Ephraim followed her in and sat next to Livy on the bench. Livy handed him her glass, but he gave it back and lay his head on the table. He was exhausted from crying. Livy downed the last of her brandy in a gulp.

"You poor, dear child," Mrs. Wilkes said, after several restorative sips. "I can only begin to imagine the insults and humiliations you have been forced to endure, living among those . . . savages."

Tipsy, Livy wondered if she was referring to Lawson or the Gunns.

"I can't change what you have been through, but I can promise you this. You will never have to see the Gunns again. They were intolerably negligent in placing you in a situation where a savage could propose to make you his . . . his . . . wife."

Mrs. Wilkes's mouth pursed, as if she'd gone for the snuff and mistakenly taken alum. She lay a hand over her heart. "You needn't fear going back. You may stay with us for as long as you wish. I swear to you, there is nothing on heaven or earth that could ever persuade me to return you to that nest of vipers."

Mr. Wilkes came in carrying a shawl. "When I think of a child of her caliber being forced into such degraded association with those red instruments of Satan, it makes my blood boil." He draped the shawl around Livy's shoulders and patted her kindly.

"Mr. Lawson may be a rascal," Mr. Wilkes continued, "but we owe him a debt of gratitude for rescuing you. I cannot believe one of those creatures actually proposed marriage! To be honest, the mere thought of you with him makes me ill. You were fortunate, Deliverance. I mean to say, I am assuming that the savage did not actually act on his evil intentions?"

Livy flinched at his words. Mrs. Wilkes looked sympathetic, but her eyes were bright with curiosity. Every grown person Livy'd been near lately seemed to have their minds stuck on Sodom and Gomorrah. They made her feel dirty. And they wanted to keep her here. To rescue her from Rising Hawk. From Rising Hawk!

She looked into the fire. There were bright blue and white tiles the entire length of the hearth. A silver tea service sparkled on a walnut sideboard. This room, with its warm fire and pretty things, had seemed like a haven, peaceful and civilized, up to this moment.

They watched her, her head down, studying the tabletop. Suddenly she stood up.

"Mr. Wilkes, Mrs. Wilkes. You have both been so kind to me and Ephraim that I feel I owe you the truth." She paused and put a corner of the shawl to her eyes. "The fact is, me and the Indian have been sinning together for, oh, I don't know how long. And now here I am, a month gone already and nearly a widow before I'm married."

Mrs. Wilkes fainted with a loud thud. Livy took a certain satisfaction in the sound.

Chapter 29

The two children were sent away at dawn, in an oxcart driven by Mr. Wilkes. In her parting words to Livy, Mrs. Wilkes expressed her hope that the jolting of the cart over the corduroy road might induce a miscarriage, thereby relieving Livy of her disgrace. Through it all Livy maintained an absolute silence, her face alternating between deep blushes and ashen pallor. Ephraim, experiencing a turmoil of his own, could barely look at her, although once in the oxcart and out of sight of Mrs. Wilkes, he did take her hand.

The sun was just rising when they met Gideon. Rising Hawk had been so frantic about her that Gideon had gone back last night, followed Livy's trail until dark, then curled up under a leaf pile until sunrise made it possible to continue. His relief at finding her safe was checked, somewhat, by Mr. Wilkes's sour greeting. "Take them, Gunn. I fervently pray I will never have to deal with either of them again."

Livy slipped out of the cart before Mr. Wilkes came to a full stop.

"Rising Hawk's hurt. I think I can find the place."

"He's safe, Livy," Gideon assured her. "It's all right. I was hunting yesterday with a friend. Rising Hawk's home, and alive." He didn't know what to make of Wilkes, who had listened, then turned the cart and started back without a word.

"Wilkes," Gideon called after him. The cart was noisy. Wilkes didn't look back. Gideon ran to catch up. Walking at the old man's side, he said, "You sent ground corn out from the mill last week. For my children, the miller's boy said. I wanted to thank you for it."

He put out his hand. Wilkes pulled up and looked down at him. Gideon still wore a bandage over the eye socket. Wilkes couldn't help but stare.

"I wouldn't want your kiddies to starve. It is not their fault they have you for a father. And the village, of course, can't condone what happened at your place." He didn't offer his hand.

Gideon flushed a little, but kept his hand out. "It was kind," he said. Reluctantly, Wilkes put his hand in Gideon's, clasped it indifferently, and took up the reins again. "And thank you and Mrs. Wilkes, for caring for these two." Gideon nodded toward Livy and Ephraim.

Wilkes snorted. "Look to them, neighbor Gunn. I almost feel the village should increase their board fee as an incentive to you to keep them out of town."

The children were staring, too. Gideon had nearly forgotten. He touched the bandage, as if he were brushing a fly. "I'll explain later. It was a fellow didn't like me much. Name of Lawson."

Livy and Eph exchanged glances.

"Ephraim," he said, putting his hands on the boy's shoulders. "I am going to ask you this once, and I want the truth. You should know that whatever you say, I intend keeping you, son, but I want to know flat out. You told that road crew about the Seneca coming and going at my place. Was it out of spite?"

Eph had been dreading this conversation for a week. He planted his feet and looked his master in the eye. "No, sir. It was out of stupidity. I was showing off. I guess I'm just getting dumber." He dropped his gaze. "I am so sorry. Did it pain you much?" he whispered.

Gideon patted Eph's shoulder and smiled grimly. "I hope you'll never know how much, son. But welcome home anyway."

Eph looked up to speak, then hid his face in Gideon's tattered shirt.

Rising Hawk was dozing in the longhouse when the hanging on his sleeping compartment ripped aside.

"A baby? What were you thinking of?"

Rising Hawk blinked owlishly at Gideon. Ephraim was standing off to the side, looking guilty.

"I had to tell them, Rising Hawk. For Livy's sake."

Rising Hawk struggled into a sitting position.

"As soon as you can stand on your own, I'm beating the stuffin' out of you," Gideon promised.

"Whose baby?"

"Livy's! The one you fathered on her. We know. She told the Wilkeses. You idiot!"

"Rising Hawk, it was the meanest thing I ever saw," Eph broke in. "One minute old Mrs. Wilkes was bleating over Livy like she was her lost lamb. The next, she's sending her to hell and back for being a fornicator. She locked her in the cellar overnight and wouldn't even let her eat breakfast in the house, but made her sit out in the yard."

"Servant girl with a bastard ain't that shocking," Gideon said grimly. "But you're an Indian, Rising Hawk. Do you have any notion of the sorrow you've brought down on that child?"

Polly looked in, one hand laid instinctively over her own flat stomach. "Rising Hawk. How could you?"

"She told them I gave her a belly?" He struggled to the edge of the bed, dragging his injured leg painfully over the side. "Brother, give me your hand," he said impatiently.

Livy woke as Rising Hawk leaned in and gently brushed her bruised cheek. She smiled sleepily when she recognized him.

"You told them we made a baby?"

"Yes."

"Knowing what would happen?"

"Yes."

"You are a most contrary girl, Livy Pelton. When I offered to show you the delights that can get a baby, you wouldn't let me."

"No."

"And you wouldn't let me now, would you?"

"No. I haven't changed my mind about that."

"You went against your village for me," he whispered. "Even though I wasn't sure I could do the same for you. You made your own people cast you out. You are a strong and wonderful woman, Livy, and braver than I'll ever be."

He crawled into her sleeping compartment and lay next to her.

"I'm not so brave, Rising Hawk," she whispered, nestling close and laying her head on his shoulder. "Those people aren't my village. You are."

Chapter 30

Polly Gunn sailed into Tyler's general store in a swirl of snow and woolen cloak, her maidservant trailing in her wake. Noah Tyler was accustomed to her monthly visits. Since late summer she had been bringing all her butter and cheese to town in payment for a rifle. Now, with dairying over, she was bringing him all the spun wool she could spare, and some lengths of linen.

At each visit, she and the little maid would stand by the hearth, eventually shedding cloaks and shawls. Mrs. Gunn had a figure worth looking at, the men who socialized at the store agreed, although each month her pregnancy became more and more obvious. But it was the maidservant they observed most closely.

Rumor had it the chit had whored with an Indian and was expecting his bastard. Now, in February, it was plain to them all that the child's belly was flat as a plank, and they lost interest. They snickered about old lady Wilkes and joked that they should build themselves some stocks and clap the old lady in them for a gossip. There was nothing worse, they all agreed, than a gossiping woman.

Livy was indifferent to the villagers' opinions. She shocked Polly, telling her she didn't give a hang, and Polly had to threaten a whipping just to make her scramble onto Ollie Rhodes's mare for the trip to town.

Rising Hawk was gone, and Livy had retreated into herself.

It was early morning on hog-butchering day when they discovered he was missing. Gideon had tried to rouse him. When he'd gotten no answer, he'd torn back the hanging of his sleeping compartment and found it empty of all traces, except for a small silver brooch. Livy recognized it as the one he wore over his heart. He had left it lying in the indentation of his pillow. She refused to touch it and went back to her work without a word, but Polly noticed by nightfall that it was gone.

The day after the butchering, Livy disappeared at dawn. There was new snow, and her trail was as clear as finger marks on foggy glass. Since she had taken nothing with her but her shawl to wrap in, they assumed she had gone for a solitary walk and would be back for breakfast.

When two hours passed without her reappearance, Gideon set off alone and found her miles from home, deep in the woods. He heard her before he saw her and was starting into a run at the shrieking until he recognized that there was no fear in her voice.

She was picking up deadfall, blindly stooping and taking whatever her hand caught at, then slamming the branches at tree trunks, over and over, until they snapped, flying back and smacking into her belly, bouncing off her shoulders, coming perilously close to her eyes. Her face twisted as she screamed, "Coward!" again and again. Gideon listened for a good while, concealed behind an elm. The silver medallion and brooch went flying past him. He marked where they landed and retrieved them silently.

When it was finally over and she lay spent and breathing hard like someone in the final stages of a deadly fever, he came to her. She lay motionless, looking up at him.

"He said he was tired of waiting. He said he'd come back one day and bring his wife and children to meet me."

Gideon knelt and took her snow-reddened hands between his own. "He was desperate, to be so cruel, Livy. He didn't mean it."

"Yes, he did. If only I weren't such a coward."

She looked near to collapse. Gideon scooped her up and held her like a baby. "Honey, me and Polly have been through three birthings by ourselves out here. No midwife. No neighbor women. No nothing. No man with experience would confuse caution with cowardice, or fault you for it, neither."

For weeks Livy spent all her spare time working silently on the loom Gideon and Eph had reconstructed in the east end of the longhouse. Years later, when the children talked about the longhouse winter, their most vivid memory was falling asleep to the steady *thwick-thwack* of Livy's loom. From her corner, Livy saw how Gideon began to spend more time indoors as Polly's lying-in time drew near. She watched him entertain the children, dandle baby Sam on his knee, rub Polly's feet at the end of the day. When the children were asleep, he'd work on the new cradle board, still attentive, retrieving Polly's dropped thimble or needles and receiving her silent thanks.

Polly never complained to Livy of Gideon, as Aunt Mary had been inclined to complain of Uncle John. They seemed to grow for each other, a tree with two trunks, their strength shifting from one branch to another, as needed. Livy's thoughts of Rising Hawk became a torment.

If it hadn't been for John Gage wintering over with them, Polly would have wondered at the falling level in the applejack barrel. Gideon knew the reason, but being aware of Polly's views, kept it to himself.

One night, not long after Rising Hawk left, he woke to see Livy at the fire pit, sitting and staring into the flames. She was sipping from a mug in her hand. After a while, she rose and walked around and around the fire, as if she were working a spell or putting herself into a trance.

The next morning she was ill, baffling everyone but Gideon and John Gage, who knew a hangover when he saw one. Neither man betrayed her, but from then on, Gideon listened for her at night. When she couldn't sleep for grief, he'd take her to the outside hearth and join her, sharing sips and cautioning her when she'd had enough.

Sometimes he'd light up and they'd share some tobacco. He'd let her talk if she was of a mind, or leave her alone if she was quiet. It was the first time he'd been nursemaid to a brokenhearted girl.

"Do you think he's married, Gideon?" Trembling, she took a long drink from the jug before handing it back.

"No. Even if he didn't love you, which he does, he's young. Seneca don't marry young."

He stared into the fire, looking solemn. Livy lifted her hand for the pipe, and he passed it without a word.

"How do you know he loves me?" It was strange how easily she could ask that question. Up to now, just using the word *love* had made her feel as if she'd gone naked to church. It was probably the darkness that made her bold.

"I know my brother. He never stays here for more than a month. He's always afraid I'll ask him to help me with the farming. Something had to be keeping him. I never thought it might be you."

Livy stared into the fire a long while. He passed her the jug.

"I blame myself," he said.

"For what?"

"For everything. All of it. For you and Rising Hawk, for this," he pointed to his eye patch. "For . . . Polly. I shouldn't have beaten Eph. That's what started the trouble. I wasn't raised to it, and it felt wrong from start to finish. When it comes to figuring the right path, I'm a blind bear in the woods. Sometimes I think being educated by Father Clairemont was a curse. When all I knew was the Seneca way, I never had to make so many decisions. Now, looking at both sides of everything has got to be a habit, and it slows me down. The only good that came of it was Polly." He took the jug from her hand and gulped. "Never, never, never do anything that goes against your gut, Deliverance."

"That doesn't work. If I'd gone with inclination, I wouldn't have stepped into that canoe. It was my head made me do it, to spite you." She lifted her hand for a drink, but he shook his head.

"You've had enough, child. You're getting philosophical."

"'T'aint fair. You're just mad 'cause I'm right. When I first met you, I thought you were the lowest creature I ever saw, and I was sure Rising Hawk was evil incarnate. That was trained into me, but it felt like gut, and it turned out to be wrong."

"You were scared of everything then."

"Yes, I was," she said, taking a deep draw on the pipe. "Only one thing scares me now."

"What's that?"

"That I'm crazy and will never get these thoughts of Rising Hawk out of my head."

By late February, only a month before the baby was due, Livy was able to sleep peacefully through the night. She gave up liquor, and she and Polly finally started talking about things she'd only discussed with Rising Hawk. She still wove ceaselessly, and spun wool and knitted, but now they talked.

"When Aunt Mary's last two babies were born, I was allowed to stay when the women gathered, but as soon as she started screaming and the birthing chair was brought out, I was sent away. No one attended her then but the midwife and the married women, but I heard enough. It made me want to scream, too."

"Don't be afraid of the screaming, Livy. That's where the strength comes from. It's plain anger."

"You don't look like you've got any mad in you, Polly." Or strength, neither, she added silently.

"Just enough," Polly said, fixing Livy with a long, serious look. "You know you'll be right in the middle of it this time—you, Eph, John, and the children. There's no place to send you."

"I know. And I'll be shamed forever if you try to worry about my weak stomach when you're going through all that."

"I'm no saint, Livy. I don't expect I'll give a good . . . goddamn about you then. Or anyone else, either."

They had a guilty moment of silence at the cussword, then collapsed against each other, howling with laughter.

Polly laid her head on Livy's shoulder and was silent a long while. "Life is never so dear as when you have children. You want to hold on to it so hard, for their sake. You can't bear to imagine them having to fend for themselves. If something goes wrong, Livy, don't leave them. Gideon wouldn't be able to bear it alone. Promise me."

Livy whispered, "I promise," as the longhouse went cold and all her fears came flooding back.

Polly labored for three hours before Gideon woke Livy. "It's hard," he said, "but that's good. I expect the baby will come by sunrise. Her water broke as soon as she stood up. She's going to get noisy now, so we'll have to take turns with the children. John's dead drunk, but Ephraim's up trying to quiet Hannah. I don't think she remembers Samuel's birth. Naturally, she thinks Mama's dying."

Livy was wild-eyed and shaking when she took Polly's arm to walk with her up and down the longhouse hall. Whenever Polly doubled up with a pain, she squeezed Livy's arm hard. By the sixth time, Livy was covered with bruises and ready to slap her loose. When Polly shrieked, "I can't bear this!" she muttered soothing words and thanked God that it wasn't her.

An hour later Polly stood with her back braced against Gideon, who held her in his arms, his back braced against the wall. Her eyes were wide with pain as she was carried along by another contraction. There was a long, muffled scream, and the harness strap she'd been gnawing fell to the floor, bit clean through.

"My God, they're coming fast," Gideon said. "You're nearly there, ain't you, darlin'? Just a few more of the bad ones, and you can go back to bed and sleep." He raised his sleeve to her forehead and wiped at the sweat. Polly caught his wrist and closed her eyes.

"You're doing fine, darlin'. Livy's back. See?"

"I poured cold water on John and kicked him and made him get up. I promised him I'd uncork the barrel and let it run out if he didn't help us. He's minding Hannah and Samuel. Eph took Henry outside for some air. Actually, it's Eph who's looking sick."

Polly caught at Livy's hand and screamed loud enough to start Gideon shaking. "Livy," he said in a voice that was hoarse and urgent. "Get the stool. Be quick now, she's near ready to drop."

Livy pried her hand loose and got it.

Gideon shut his eyes against the next scream and slid onto the low stool, lowering Polly gently onto his lap as he did. She let out a moan.

Livy knelt at Polly's feet, suddenly weak and dizzy at what she was seeing. She fought an impulse to be sick. "Polly, I can see the baby's head." Her voice came from far away, but it was calm and steady.

"Push, Polly," Gideon whispered. "You can push now. You're almost done."

It was terrifying and wonderful, seeing them locked together like that. Polly wrapped her legs around his. Gideon braced himself, his legs wide to open hers while her ankles dug into his calves and her toenails cut him. Polly's gasps turned to bellows, and her face twisted hideously in a push. Livy focused all her attention on the baby, laying hold and supporting it gently as Polly gave another holler and a shove, then another, and another as the baby slowly squeezed out of her and into Livy's hands.

He was slimy and warm, with a tiny face like bloody, kneaded dough, and he smelled, revoltingly, of pork sausage. Livy laid him in her lap, and felt her shift soaking up blood and water and the white, caulky stuff that coated him.

"Is it all right?" Polly said, in a voice heavy with fatigue.

Even in the dim light of the banked fire, Livy could see webs of broken blood vessels on her eyelids. The longhouse was full of the smells of Polly's sweat and blood, but she was smiling. Gideon's face was bent to hers as he kissed her over and over, trembling with relief.

"He's perfect. Absolutely beautiful," Livy said, as the tiny creature in her arms jerked and began to wail. She felt a sudden surge of energy, a joy so intense that her fingers and toes tingled. The tension and fear of all the hours before melted away. Anything seemed possible. "This is what you meant, isn't it, Rising Hawk?" she whispered. "We don't seem worthy of it somehow, this kind of joy. But this must be how it's always been. 'These are the generations of the heavens and of the earth.'" Tears mingled with the mess in her lap as she offered the baby up to his parents.

Chapter 31

"Livy." Gideon's sleepy voice cut into a dream where she'd been soaring over treetops, then dipping lower, staying just above the curious hands of the people on the ground. "Baby's crying. Polly nursed him less than an hour ago. Walk him, won't you? Outside, please. It's nearly light."

Livy groaned with exasperation and pulled herself out of bed. Baby Isaac was a month old and colicky. He hadn't slept through the night even once and had a knack for waking thirteen-month-old Samuel, who would howl along. Like a couple of wolf cubs, Livy thought bitterly.

Outside the moon still lit the clearing. It was nowhere near dawn, and the wet penetrated Livy's moccasins as she walked around the fire pit, holding the baby first over her shoulder, then cradled in her arms. Frustrated, she sat and laid him facedown on her knees and rubbed the little back until the squalling and jerking subsided into slumber. As soon as the baby had quieted, Livy forgave him for her interrupted sleep and the cold and damp.

Her euphoria at the baby's birth had been nearly overwhelming. She remembered being happy with the birth of each new cousin, but not like this. Something had got free, and even though the reality of caring for two squalling infants may have tamed the euphoria, nothing could extinguish her joy. Similarly, Livy's hunger for Rising Hawk, inflamed by the baby's birth, had dwindled but was still there, quietly alive like the smoldering fire at her feet.

Meanwhile, Polly was nursing two babies and having a slow recovery. Gideon was busy reconstructing their cabin and trying to plant the first corn crop. Already there was tension between them because Polly insisted he sleep alone, and Gideon couldn't very well refuse, considering.

Later that morning, John Gage and Eph went down to the homestead right after breakfast. The walls of the new cabin were up, managed between plowing and planting, and they were eager to raise the roof. Eph, who had grown in Gideon's estimation over the winter, had assumed a gently teasing authority over John and kept him sober most of April.

Gideon stayed behind, watching Livy wash up. He prowled back and forth for some time before he said, "Livy, I got to talk to you, man to man." Since the nights spent draining the applejack, he'd taken to treating her like a little brother, going so far as to give her a cast-off pair of breeches and threatening to take her hunting as soon as Polly could spare her. "Are you still hungering after my worthless brother?"

Livy finished drying the samp kettle and calmly said, "No." Gideon folded his arms and stood looking at her for the longest time. "What are you studying me for?" she said when the silence had grown uncomfortable and she had the fleeting ridiculous thought that deprivation was about to drive him to an improper amorous advance.

"I'm trying to decide if you're lying to me or not."

"You know I don't lie."

"Not about most things, but you do about yourself. Hell, Livy, the only time you've ever been entirely truthful about your own personal self was when you'd been drinking."

She frowned. He was only partially right. "It's not that I lie on purpose, Gideon. I can't seem to catch at things. Just when I think I know what I want, it's out of my hands like a fish, back in that murky water, and I have to feel around for it all over again."

"This won't help clear the waters any," Gideon said reluctantly. "I had a message the other day. Rising Hawk's planning another visit. I knew you'd want a warning." As usual, the expression on her face told him absolutely nothing.

———

"It's simple," Polly said. "Do you love him? You'll be sixteen in August. That's young, but you are the oldest child I ever met. Do you love him?"

"Everyone's always saying that. It's not simple."

"You're thinking too much again, Livy."

And some people don't think enough, Livy thought as she glanced down at baby Isaac in Polly's arms. But all she said was, "Maybe."

First she saw light, the rising sun reflecting off something at the clearing's edge. In that moment before she heard the voices, she confusedly thought she was seeing fireflies in the daytime, then realized it was silver brooches catching the light. No one had told her to expect the family, but there they were: Rising Hawk's uncle, his parents, and assorted cousins, including Dream Teller, who gave Livy a tight smile she took for a peace offering. Rising Hawk lagged behind, carrying a scrawny deer over his shoulders, his eyes focused on the path. The others had the good sense and tact to pass on with a simple greeting, but Buffalo Creek Woman put her hands to Livy's chest and with a stream of words, finally cut short by Cold Keeper, forgave her everything.

When the company had passed on, Rising Hawk laid the deer carcass on the ground at her feet. "This is for Polly," he said shyly. "It is unthinkable for a bridegroom to claim his bride without proof of his hunting skill. The deer around here are not well. Your winter must have been bad, like ours. This was the best I could find." His eyes finally met hers. He was the same, a little haggard. She was older. Neither of them was sure that they read anything in the looks they gave each other. "Gideon gave you my message? I was afraid it would not get here before I did."

"He told me yesterday," she said, "but he didn't tell me you were bringing a wedding party." She was cool, without anger, very polite—as if she were addressing an acquaintance, and a distant one at that. Rising Hawk felt his confidence melting away.

"Why didn't you send word sooner?" she asked, her voice accusing.

"I tried, but there was no one to take my message, once I had the courage to try. Anyway, there seemed to be no words for my sorrow that you had not heard before."

"Oh."

He was beginning to think he had made a mistake. This was shaping up as a refusal. And after all the persuading he had wasted on his uncle and grandmother. He glanced down at the deer. It was humiliating, but he hadn't come all this way to stand here dumb, like a chastened twelve-year-old. Without raising his eyes he said, "I missed you so much my soul was sick. My only dreams were of you. On the winter hunt my aim was terrible, like an old man with fading sight. My friends pitied me. I could listen to stories in the longhouse, but I could not tell any afterward because my heart held no memory of them." He paused, ashamed to admit it. "I tried drinking for a while."

He saw her start slightly, and she said, less harshly, "Me, too."

"What happened between us was my fault."

"No, it wasn't. I said I wouldn't marry you. What else could I expect? Your only fault was in leaving without saying good-bye. That made it terrible."

"I'm sorry, Livy. I behaved like a spiteful boy."

"Yes, you did."

She agreed much too easily, he thought. She might be more gracious about it. "My uncle was right. A man should never meddle in women's affairs."

"What do you mean?"

"I mean that it was foolish of me to speak to you of marriage. Only an older woman would have known how to calm your fears."

"No amount of talk from anyone could do that, Rising Hawk. I wish it would," she admitted with a sigh.

He reached for her hands. He pulled gently, but she set her heels and wouldn't budge, so he did. Coming as close as he dared, he whispered, "Do you remember our last day at Jenuchshadego? You fought like a demon."

"It wasn't just me. We all went crazy."

"But you most of all."

She laughed, and he remembered how desolate winter had been without her.

"You fought like a demon. Everyone was astonished. Me most of all. The violence of your tongue I was used to, but this! When it was over, you rose from the floor and looked at me."

She laughed again. It was like a familiar birdsong, lost for the winter, now returned.

"And at that moment, the light of your eyes went into mine, and mine into yours in return." Timidly, he touched her cheek, and felt ready to cry with relief when she raised her hand and touched his.

"That sounds very pretty, Rising Hawk," she said gently, "but it's not enough to trade my life for."

"Livy, we both know that once this happens, one is blind without the other. What do you need for proof? Another winter like this past one? Listen, I never would have come back like this, been so sure, if something hadn't happened to make me realize I had to. That *you* wanted me to."

"What do you mean? Don't tell me about another dream, Rising Hawk, because I don't believe in them."

"This was not a dream. Just a moon ago, at dawn, I was drunk. Very drunk. I wasn't thinking of you. You were the last thing on my mind. I was trying to get up from where I lay on the riverbank without falling in. I couldn't tell the water from the sky. I was seeing two skies and two rivers and knew that if I took a wrong step I would probably drown, and I was deciding whether or not that would be a bad thing. The next thing I knew I was in the center of the river on that flat rock you used to sit on, and I looked up into the sky, and suddenly my vision cleared. I knew that you wanted me back. I knew, at that moment, we were both seeing into your heart."

She didn't tell him that was probably the morning the baby came, but he saw her struggle and her resignation and her surprise. There's no real reason for this, she thought. There's no good reason. I can't believe such nonsense, but it happened. I don't know my own mind even now when he's standing right in front of me, so dear, so beautiful, and much too good. Much too good. Why can't I have his faith?

Rising Hawk watched her face, and he began to believe that if he could just touch her, kiss her the way he had on the trail, she would give in. But then she said, "Rising Hawk. Would you do something for me?"

Her voice suggested some new torment. His vulnerable expression fled. He wasn't going to be made to look like a fool. Not even by Livy, no matter how dear she was to him. He thought about the winter. She made him laugh. Most of the time, she made him happy. They all believed she still had him bewitched. Maybe she did. Against his better judgment and his gut feeling, he felt himself nod yes.

She took a deep breath. "Turn around and walk away."

"What?"

"Turn around and walk away." She had done all the thinking she could. By itself it held no answers. This was her last chance.

"That's what you want?"

"Yes."

His next words had to fight their way out. His teeth were set like a bear trap. "I don't know why I love you. It never makes any sense to me. Nothing about you does." He turned.

Livy watched him walk away. His familiar stride, the way he held his head, and the slight limp helped her remember the trail, their strange journey, and the gunshot. It's not fair, she told herself as the pain of seeing him walk away one last time took hold of her.

"It's not enough," she said aloud in an angry sob that rose in her throat and nearly choked her next words. "But I can't help it. I can't, and I don't care anymore. I don't care. Rising Hawk, wait!" she called, and broke into a run. He slowed at the sound of her voice and looked over his shoulder. The old smile returned to his face, gentle, mocking, assured. He didn't wait for her to reach him, but turned to meet her halfway.

A Glossary of People, Places, and Concepts

LIEUTENANT THOMAS BOYD: The unfortunate lieutenant who was one of the sixteen or so American troops killed on the Sullivan expedition. He was captured and tortured to death along with Sergeant Michael Parker at a Seneca village called Genesee Castle. Livy's uncle would have been part of that expedition and told her the story.

JOSEPH BRANT: A prominent Mohawk statesman who fought with the British during the American Revolution. Following the war, he was a spokesperson for the Six Nations in Canada. He envisioned an Indian confederation to protect the interests of all Indian people in dealing with the American expansion.

COLONEL JOHN BUTLER, WALTER BUTLER, AND SIR JOHN JOHNSON: During the American Revolution, these men led New York Loyalist militias consisting of American Tories, British regular army volunteers, and Indians, largely of the Mohawk and Seneca nations. These forces were instrumental in the battles at Wyoming and Cherry Valley, both of which terrified New York settlers as accounts of the atrocities committed against American rebels spread. In this novel, Livy's uncle fought against these militias.

CANNIBALISM: In North America and worldwide, many tribal peoples once practiced a ritualistic cannibalism in which parts of an enemy were cooked and eaten. It is believed that the purpose was to consume and thus acquire the good qualities of a brave opponent. By the time of the Revolutionary War, this practice seems to have been abandoned by the Six Nations.

CHERRY VALLEY: This was a New York town, also the site of an American fort, that was attacked in 1778 by a force of Tories, British regular army volunteers, and some Six Nations warriors. There was a massacre of noncombatants. Thirty women and children were killed, possibly in revenge for the destruction of two abandoned Mohawk towns at Oquaga and Unadilla by American forces.

CLANS: There are eight clans within the Seneca nation. Only three of these clans—Turtle, Wolf, and Bear—are present in all of the original five nations. Clan members trace their origins back to one common ancestor.

CORNPLANTER: A Seneca war chief who became an important spokesperson for the Seneca in the years following the end of the Revolutionary War. In addition to trying to maintain Seneca neutrality while standing between warring western tribes and the United States government, Cornplanter addressed Congress and corresponded with President Washington, asking for help in modernizing the Seneca economy. By 1813, Seneca women were producing a surplus in woolen and linen cloth, which they sold to the white settlers.

PETER CROUSE: A white captive who was adopted by the Seneca as a boy. The Haudenosaunee culture relied heavily on adoption of outsiders to replace warriors killed in battle and deceased family members. At the time of our story, Peter Crouse was one of the few English speakers living among the Seneca people. He was also one of several examples of captives who had opportunities to move back into white culture but who preferred the Seneca.

GENESEE TOWNS: A reference to Seneca villages on the upper and lower Genesee River. These were the first Seneca towns to be surrounded by white settlements. Historians suggest that often the earliest frontiersmen were not the most scrupulous or law-abiding people and served as poor ambassadors for further settlers. In other words, they brought alcohol and were violent and uncivilized.

SIMON GIRTY: As a boy, he spent several years among the Seneca as a captive and sometimes served as an interpreter. He was a Tory who earned a reputation for cruelty by encouraging the torture of American prisoners. He was also involved in the war in Ohio Territory against the Americans and was eager to urge the western tribes to war.

HAUDENOSAUNEE: This term is translated several ways. Each translation tends to be a variation on "the people of the longhouse" and refers to the Six Nations. The French derived the term *Iroquois* from an Algonquian word for this same group of tribes.

INDIAN TRADE AND INTERCOURSE ACT OF 1790: This federal law made all sales of Indian land illegal unless approved by the United States government. This and similar laws were attempts to stop New York State from engaging in questionable land deals with the Six Nations.

IROQUOIS CONFEDERACY: The political organization of the Haudenosaunee, based on the Great Binding Law, which still governs the Iroquois today. Believed to have originated in the fifteenth century, the confederacy consists of the Mohawk, Oneida, Onondaga, Cayuga, and Seneca nations.

JENUCHSHADEGO: The town given to Cornplanter by the United States government to belong to the Seneca "forever." Evidently that word is open to interpretation. In 1964 Jenuchshadego was taken back by the federal government for the construction of Kinzua Dam.

MATRILINEAL: In a matrilineal society, descent is traced through the mother's side of the family. Iroquois children belong to their mother's clan. Traditionally, when a couple married, the husband usually went to live with his wife's family.

MAUMEE COUNCIL: There is an oral tradition among the Seneca that says that Cornplanter and his party went to a council held by the western tribes on the Maumee River in the spring of 1793. The members of the Seneca party were treated with open contempt for their attempts to stay neutral and were held against their will. Finally released, they made for home, and some of their party died on the way. It is believed that they were poisoned.

PAUPER'S AUCTION: Because premature death was relatively common, Pauper's Auctions were a practical way to provide for poor women and children who had lost the support of their extended families. How carefully the paupers were disposed of is anybody's guess.

PHELPS AND GORHAM: In 1788 Oliver Phelps and Nathaniel Gorham purchased two and a half million acres of Seneca land, which stretched from Seneca Lake in the east to the Genesee River in the west. Later they formed the Phelps and Gorham Land Company and sold the land in parcels.

RED JACKET: A Seneca orator considered the best in the confederacy. At the Glaize Indian council in September 1792, he spoke for five hours, trying to persuade the warring western confederacy to make peace with the Americans. He was not a supporter of the Americans but feared the destructive power of a new war that he thought was probably not winnable. His plea was rejected.

SACHEM: A sachem is a civil chief. There are fifty such hereditary offices distributed among the original Five Nations. Sachems maintain order and calm and serve as a counterbalance for the power of the warriors and the women. They are referred to as Confederate Lords in the Great Binding Law and make up the Confederate Council. A sachem is expected to display patience, selflessness, goodwill, and restraint.

LIEUTENANT GOVERNOR JOHN GRAVES SIMCOE: A British colonel who was appointed the lieutenant governor of Upper Canada in 1791. He feared American expansion as much as the Indians did. During the turmoil of the 1790s, he tried using diplomacy and manipulation to establish an Indian territory to separate the borders of Canada and the United States.

SIX NATIONS: In the early 1700s the Tuscarora nation lost its territory in North Carolina and migrated north to Pennsylvania and New York. It was adopted into the confederacy by the Oneidas. Since then, the Haudenosaunee have been the Six Nations and include the Mohawk, Oneida, Onondaga, Cayuga, Seneca, and Tuscarora.

GENERAL ARTHUR ST. CLAIR: An American general who was sent to establish a fort in hostile Miami territory. During this expedition on November 4, 1791, he lost half his army in a battle with tribes of the western confederacy, chiefly Shawnee and Miami. This Indian victory gave strength to the western tribes who wanted to fight to keep Americans out of Ohio.

GENERALS SULLIVAN AND CLINTON: American generals commanding the force that swept through Indian country in the Finger Lakes region of New York in 1779, burning villages, crops, and food stores. The campaign was in retaliation for raids against New Yorkers on the frontier.

TOWN DESTROYER: The name given to George Washington by the Seneca for sending the armies of Generals Sullivan and Clinton to burn their villages, crops, and food stores. One survivor said that the Indians were left destitute in the coldest winter she had ever seen. Many died in the harsh conditions.

UPPER CANADA: English-speaking Canada, located above the Ottawa River. French-speaking Canada was below the river.

WESTERN TRIBES: At the time of this story, American settlers, both legal and illegal, were beginning to invade Indian lands in Ohio. There was a loose confederacy of western tribes trying to stop American expansion at the Ohio River. Among those tribes were the Shawnee, Miami, Kickapoo, Huron, Chippewa, Ottawa, Potawatomi, Delaware, Cherokee, Creek, Mingo, and Wyandot.

WITCHCRAFT: In the 1790s witches and their evil influence were blamed for all kinds of misfortune among the Haudenosaunee people, as a folk belief in witchcraft continued to flourish in various white communities. One eyewitness said that there was a witch executed by the Seneca every year for thirty years. When a culture is in the middle of violent and wrenching social change, as the Seneca were, the hunt for scapegoats tends to increase.

A Note about Seneca Names

The Seneca names in our story are fictitious. Authentic names are sacred and belong to the clans. They are bestowed by the clan mothers over the generations so that every name has a history. Besides being disrespectful, using one would be like naming a character George Washington without actually meaning *that* George Washington. The names also tend to be long and unwieldy in English translation. For example, Joseph Brant's Mohawk name was Thayendanegea, which apparently translates as "two sticks of wood bound together." And they may be difficult to pronounce. The names I have used have come from reading Seneca myths and history and are my attempts to reflect the culture without being disrespectful. If any of the fictitious names are similar to actual names, it is purely coincidental.